GRAMPA LEARY

GRAMPA LEARY

A MEREDITH, MASSACHUSETTS NOVEL

J.A. McINTOSH

Visit our website at **www.StillwaterPress.com** for more information.

First Stillwater River Publications Edition.

ISBN: 978-1-955123-88-4

1 2 3 4 5 6 7 8 9 10
Written by J.A. McIntosh.
Interior book design by Matthew St. Jean.
Published by Stillwater River Publications, Pawtucket, RI, USA.

For Tony.

LEARY/VEGA FAMILY

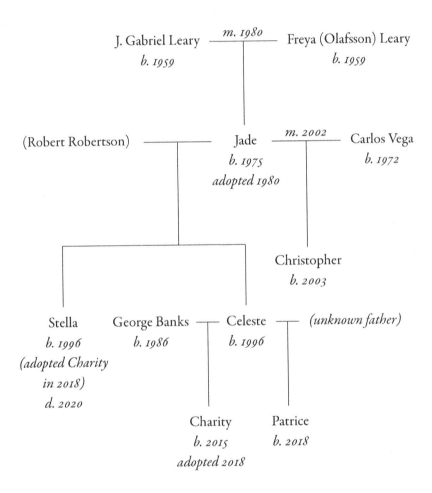

J. Gabriel Leary — *m. 1980* — Freya (Olafsson) Leary
b. 1959   *b. 1959*

(Robert Robertson) — Jade — *m. 2002* — Carlos Vega
b. 1975   *b. 1972*
adopted 1980

Christopher
b. 2003

Stella   George Banks — Celeste — (unknown father)
b. 1996   *b. 1986*   *b. 1996*
(adopted Charity
in 2018)
d. 2020

Charity   Patrice
b. 2015   *b. 2018*
adopted 2018

Jesus Gabriel Leary (Gabe): Married to Freya (Olafsson) Leary; adopted father of Jade (Leary) Vega; grandfather of Celeste and Stella Leary (twins) and Christopher Vega; great-grandfather of Charity and Patrice Leary (children of Celeste)

Freya (Olafsson) Leary: Married to Gabe Leary; adoptive mother of Jade (Leary) Vega; grandmother of Celeste and Stella Leary (twins) and Christopher Vega; great-grandmother of Charity and Patrice Leary (children of Celeste)

Jade (Leary) Vega: Adopted by Gabe and Freya Leary (paternal aunt and uncle); married to Carlos Vega; mother of Celeste and Stella Leary (father is Robert Robertson) and Christopher Vega (father is Carlos Vega); grandmother of Charity and Patrice (children of Celeste)

Celeste Leary: Daughter of Jade (Leary) Vega; twin of Stella Leary; half-sister of Christopher Vega; mother of Charity (father is George Banks; Charity was adopted by Celeste's twin, Stella) and Patrice Leary (father unknown)

Stella Leary: Daughter of Jade Leary; twin of Celeste Leary; half-sister of Christopher Vega; died in 2020; adopted her sister's child, Charity

Christopher Vega: Child of Jade (Leary) Vega and Carlos Vega; half-brother of twins Celeste and Stella

Charity Leary: Child of Celeste Leary and George Banks; adopted by her maternal aunt, Stella Leary, who died in 2020; half-sister of Patrice Leary

Patrice Leary: Child of Celeste Leary and unknown father; half-sister of Charity Leary

MONDAY

MARCH 9, 2020

CHAPTER ONE

FREYA

I HAVE SOME CLAIRVOYANT POWERS, BUT I DIDN'T NEED them to see that the guards at the courthouse were on alert. Guess that happens once somebody smuggles a gun into the building.

Tracy approached the security check. I decided to call her Tracy because she inserted herself into my family and I'm not going to call her Attorney Christensen, not after what she did. The guards made her dump everything out and they went through her purse and her coat. She walked through the metal detector and it started buzzing. Raising her pant leg, she showed off the metal and plastic monitor around her ankle. Even if you bring a gun into the courthouse, you get to go home on a monitor if you're a lawyer and your parents can raise half a million for bail. The largest guard made her stop and waved the black and yellow wand over her. A female guard patted her down. Guess daddy's money only gets you so far.

Though Tracy's crime included my great-granddaughter, Charity, I had to read about it in the papers. Charity's biological father, George Banks, got out of jail and wanted custody. His lawyer, Tracy Christensen, brought a gun into the courthouse and Banks used it to threaten a judge. Banks is in jail and Tracy's on a monitor.

She picked up her things at the other side of the metal detector, came over to where I was standing, and stared at me.

"I'm sorry about the death of your granddaughter, Stella."

She looked sincere, but I had reason to doubt her.

"Thank you," I said.

"We need to talk about Charity," she said. As if there was any other reason I would meet with her. "Walk with me."

I'd agreed to this meeting because I wanted to keep custody of my great-granddaughters, Charity and Patrice. Tracy's boyfriend, George Banks, just filed for custody; he's Charity's biological father and a whole lot of other things. I still don't trust Tracy. I need to talk to her about settling this thing, as our money for lawyers is running out, but I'm not going to wander through the courthouse with her.

Tracy turned toward me. "I only have ninety minutes to see my probation officer and get back to the house before the ankle monitor goes off. So, we need to walk and talk if I'm going to get everything done and get home in time." She glanced at the security officers, still watching her. "The conference rooms are on the top floors and I want some privacy to talk."

The Worcester courthouse reminded me of a mall, with a central court and corridors going up four stories. People lean against the barriers on the second and third stories and I'm always worried that someone will throw something on my head as I come into the lobby.

We walked into the elevator, empty except for us. Tracy pushed the button for the fourth floor and turned around to face me. "How is Charity doing?" she asked.

"You're not related to Charity," I said. "Just another woman in her father's life. I don't have to talk to you."

"But you might want to," she said. "Because George listens to me. It might make a difference in whether Charity stays with you and how often George gets to see her. Or, if I really wanted to, I might have Charity removed from your home."

"That's what the courts are for," I said. I'd been through this before, with Charity's biological mother, Celeste. And she cared about Charity. Not like Banks who got out of jail and wanted an instant family, then ended up back in jail after threatening a judge. We'd been studied by probation, by the Department of Children and Families, and by assorted psychologists and social workers. Everybody said the girls should stay with us.

"You're not that naïve," she said. The elevator stopped and the door opened onto the third floor. Nobody stood there. The doors closed.

"George is her father and I can tell him what to say to see Charity," Tracy continued. "You're the great-grandmother, but her father has more rights."

I swallowed the nasty words I wanted to say. "Charity has lived with us all her life, even when she was in Stella's custody. We're the only family she knows."

"And now Stella is dead, and custody is an open question."

We got out on the fourth floor.

"I want to talk about working something out so all the family can see and spend time with Charity," Tracy said.

"What do you have in mind?" If I had anything to say, Charity wasn't leaving my house. And she wasn't going with a woman who just hooked up with Charity's father a year ago. I'm not sure why she's doing this. Maybe because she's always gotten everything she wants, maybe just because she can.

"George has filed for custody."

I nodded. I got the papers a few days ago.

"Let's go in here." Tracy held open the door and we went into a conference room. "George wants to see Charity, wants to be part of her life. To be able to take her to a park, come to family events, and maybe, in the future, she can come to his house to visit."

This time, I didn't trust myself to talk.

"So, you agree that would be a good idea? I can draw up a visitation schedule, file it with the court, and we could gradually increase the time George spends with Charity."

I found my voice. "No. And you're not even a lawyer anymore."

"Just no? Can't we talk about it?"

"The judge gave us custody of Charity. Now that her biological mother's in rehab and her adopted mother is dead, he said that Charity should stay in the only home she's ever had. And I'm not taking the girls to visit their father in jail."

Tracy stared at me. "George may be released soon. And I could make a case that you raised your granddaughters, Celeste and Stella, so you are unfit to raise Charity. Celeste is a druggie, in and out of rehab, and Stella's dead. You did a great job of raising them."

I'd sometimes doubted myself, but I cared more about the girls than this woman ever would. "Being poor isn't our fault," I said. "Having to work to support the kids and Gabe getting injured at work isn't our fault. We did the best we could and it was good enough for the judge." Her first sentence registered, a little late. "And what do you mean George is getting out of jail? He brought a gun into the courthouse and threatened a judge."

"Not just poor, but your daughter, Jade, missing for almost a year; one granddaughter dead and the other, Celeste, in rehab; and trying to raise toddlers at your age." Tracy tapped the table. "George and I want a family, and that includes Charity. George was under duress and made a dumb decision. I could argue that he only wanted his child back, and the judge had the power to do that."

Not that Tracy and George were angels. "You're on a monitoring bracelet, George is in jail, and you want to raise the girls. I think I could make a case that we're the best alternative. Even if I'm not a lawyer. Of course, right now, you're not a lawyer either."

This time, I hit her where it hurt. Or maybe I just made her angry.

"And what about Celeste's other daughter, Patrice?" Tracy asked.

"What about Patrice?" I asked. "She's with us too, but she isn't Banks's child."

"You don't know that." Tracy's phone pinged and she ignored it. Guess she wasn't in such a hurry, after all. "George wasn't in jail when Patrice was conceived, he could be her father. I'll recommend that he file for custody of Patrice also."

"Patrice is only nineteen months old, lives with us, and we have custody." Not exactly true, but we'd filed for temporary orders. Celeste just dropped her off one day, said she was going to rehab, and we've been providing for her since. "Besides, George would never get past the paternity tests."

"We don't need paternity testing if Celeste agrees that he is the father. She would do that if I offered a visitation agreement to her."

They wouldn't even need that much. Celeste would sign for a handful of oxy. "I'll insist on paternity testing. So will my husband."

"I don't have time for all this family drama." Tracy pulled out her phone. "I have to go meet with my probation officer. I'm working on getting George out of jail. Talk it over with your husband and let me know what you want to do." She left.

I went back downstairs and outside. I needed coffee. But it was downtown Worcester and all the coffee around here costs five dollars a cup. I had five dollars, but I needed a dollar to take the bus back home. Because of Tracy's probation, we'd met in Worcester, rather than the local courthouse.

I walked to the bus stop and got on. The steps seemed higher than usual. Some millennial was sprawled across three seats. I pushed his leg aside and sat down. He glared at me but didn't say anything.

I got home, hot and angry, and decided I really did need a cup of coffee. I buy Dunkin' Donuts coffee, ground, by the pound. It's two dollars off every Monday and I need an indulgence. I put the coffee in the machine and turned it on.

My husband, Gabe, had gone out with Patrice, and Charity was in preschool, so I had the house to myself. Glad I didn't have to explain what I'd done to my husband just yet. I'd tried to get things resolved and might have just made Tracy angrier. Not a good start. I needed to get a grip on what might happen next.

I took the hard, smooth stones out of the velvet Crown Royal bag

I keep them in. My runes are made of amethyst, cool and hard. Gabe bought these for me on our first anniversary. That's Gabe—doesn't approve of my divinations, but he buys me the lovely runes. I have a second set, made of tan stone, that belonged to my mother and grandmother before her, but I prefer the ones Gabe bought.

I didn't know how much time I had until I'd be interrupted, so I laid out a simple four-stone pattern. Past, present, future, and a guide. The first rune was Ehwaz. The rune for the past and the rune I'd come to associate with the twins. My granddaughters were twins no more; Stella died a few weeks ago while Celeste was in rehab. They were certainly shaping our immediate past actions as we attempted to deal with Celeste's children, Charity and Patrice. I turned over the smooth stone in my hands. Stella wasn't coming back; I needed to get on with this. Maybe Stella was watching over us, making sure the girls were in a good place.

The next rune was the Thorn, symbol of the ice god, the destroyer. My family had been in chaos recently, after the upheaval of Stella's death. Most of the upheaval was about the kids. But Banks wanted to be a father and our granddaughter, Celeste, wanted to be a mother again. I said a silent prayer that the upheaval had stopped, though the fact it remained in the present position was not a good sign.

I heard the door slam and Patrice raced into the kitchen.

"Food!" yelled Patrice.

"Where did you come from?" I asked.

"Bumpa." This from Patrice.

Gabe, my husband and Patrice's Bumpa, came into the room, went to the refrigerator, and handed the girl a piece of cheese. "Now go into the other room with your food while I talk to Granny."

Patrice jumped around the kitchen for a moment, ran around the table where I sat, and raced through the open arch into the living room. I heard the television click on.

Gabe sat down across from me. "Trying to figure out where we're going from here?" He picked up the Thorn, turned it over, and put it back on the table. "You know I don't like you doing this work of the devil."

I returned the rune to its place in front of me. "You know you're not supposed to handle my runes," I said. "They need my energy to work."

"I bought them for you. I've lived with you for forty years. They probably have my energy all over them."

I shrugged. He may have a point.

His calloused, reddened finger pointed to the Thorn. "That means chaos, doesn't it? Like we don't have enough to deal with."

Shrieks came from the living room. He got up and looked in. "Sit down and eat your cheese."

"You want to talk to me about something?" I asked.

He was doing his "grumpy grampa" act, but his heart didn't seem to be in it.

"Oh, yeah." He pulled out the phone and put it on the table. "I got a call from Carlos.

He wants me to do an emergency run this afternoon." He brought the phone closer to his face. "Says we only have twenty minutes left on the plan. Maybe we should get two phones, one for each of us."

"We can't afford two phones." This was an argument we had on a weekly basis and I always won.

He returned it to his pocket. He didn't seem in a hurry to leave.

"Are we still going to the cemetery on Wednesday? Visit Stella's grave." We went every week. I doubt he'd forget.

"I know. I told Carlos I'd be there after the cemetery visit. Asked him if he wanted to come, visit his stepdaughter's grave. He said no."

I drew another rune from the bag. Wynn, symbol of my daughter Jade, the mother of the twins, Celeste and Stella; I knew that was her rune the day we got her. She'd been missing for a year, how did she come to be in the future position? Maybe she would return. I contemplated the three runes, in a line before me.

"What do you see?" asked Gabe.

"The twins, chaos, and Jade," I replied. Stella's dead, Celeste said she's in rehab, that's chaos for you. Throw in their mother, Jade, and it's not good.

"What does it mean?"

"Not sure. I haven't seen Wynn, for Jade, in a long time."

"Not for eleven months," he said. We both knew exactly how long it had been since Jade took off.

"Not for eleven months and three days," I said. "Wonder why the rune showed up now."

"Seems like most of the chaos is because of the kids, not the adults." Gabe stood up, went to the sink, and poured himself a glass of water.

"Seems so."

"Want one of these?" Gabe pointed to the glass in his hand.

No," I said. "I started coffee; then forgot about it."

Gabe went to the machine, poured a cup for each of us, and put mine in front of me. "Why don't the children show up in the runes? So much of what's going on involves them."

I took a sip. "Their personalities aren't formed yet. They are mostly at the whim of the adults."

"And the adults have really screwed things up." Gabe took the seat across from me again. "Stella dying, Celeste and Banks both wanting Charity." He took another sip of water. "At least the children landed with us."

"I want to talk to you about that. I met with Tracy Christensen this morning."

Gabe's head came up as if pulled by the hair. "What the hell did you do that for?"

"Because she asked me." That didn't really answer his question.

"Okay, why the hell didn't you take me with you?"

I was second-guessing my decision. I'd thought I'd be more reasonable than Gabe, but it didn't turn out that way. "Because I knew you'd be upset. And I wanted to know what she would say. Thought maybe I could settle this mess."

"And did you?" Gabe seemed somewhat calmer, though he turned the coffee cup in his hands.

"No. She said she wanted to make an agreement, to let George visit and maybe take Charity to his house. Thought we could save some legal fees."

"What happened?"

"Nothing. She threatened to take custody of Patrice too."

"Patrice isn't Banks's kid. "

"That's what I told her. She threatened to take both kids unless I agreed to let George see Charity." I took a swallow of coffee. It was cold. "Guess I screwed that up."

"Next time, take me with you."

As if that would make things better.

"Bumpa, Bumpa, Bumpa." Patrice ran in from the other room. She smelled.

"I'll change her pants, give me a minute," said Gabe.

"No, it's my turn." I stood up and started toward the living room.

Gabe scooped up the runes, put them in the Crown Royal bag, and put them on top of the refrigerator where the children couldn't get to them. I appreciated the gesture, but again felt he shouldn't be touching my runes.

I went into the living room. I picked up Patrice and took her into the hallway to change her diaper. Gabe followed me.

"We need to finish our conversation," he said.

I got the wipes and the clean diaper and put them on the changing table. Maybe ignoring him would work.

"What else did you and Tracy talk about?" Gabe asked.

I told him. "She wanted to upset me," I said.

"And she succeeded," Gabe went on. "You think we could lose both kids."

TUESDAY

MARCH 10, 2020

CHAPTER TWO

GABE

Bill, the owner of the QuikMart, stacked another bottle of dishwashing liquid by the door. We stepped inside and almost hit him. Some kind of contest was in progress and the windows were covered in children's drawings, so I didn't see him until I opened the door. He looked at us and said, "Hi, Patrice" to my great-granddaughter. She smiled and waved.

I pulled out the list that Freya gave me, one of her "if you're going to the store anyway" scribbles. I knew we were out of bread and orange juice. Patrice wiggled out of the stroller, ran up to one of the carts shaped like a car and climbed in. Guess we were taking that cart. She kept turning the wheel and waving to the people who passed. I leaned the stroller against the wall, picked up the bread and orange juice, and looked at the list again to see what else Freya thought we needed. I was trying to decipher Freya's handwriting, still a mystery after all these years, when my phone beeped. I took it out of my pocket and glanced at the screen. Nobody I wanted to talk to.

Someone came up behind me, so I looked up and attempted to move the cart. Patrice wasn't in it. I looked up and down the aisle and she wasn't there either. I glanced at the list for only a few moments, how far could she have gone? Bill's store is only about twenty feet wide but it extends fifty feet back from the street. Standing near the coolers, where I was, the door's behind me and to the left. Patrice couldn't have walked by me; I would have seen her. I'm very careful about where the kids are and take care that they're never alone.

I walked to the end of the aisle, past Bill, now stacking some generic sugar cereal, and scanned the front of the store. "Bill, did you see Patrice come by here?"

"Patrice?" Bill pushed the last box into place and looked up at me.

"Yes, my great-granddaughter, Patrice," I said. "She got out of the cart; I can't find her."

"I'm sure she's around here somewhere." Bill stood up and flattened the now-empty carton that had held a dozen cereal cartons.

"She could be injured, or run out into the street, or somebody could take her right out of the store," I said. "I need to find her, now. How many people are working here? Can they help me look?"

"It's just me and the kid," said Bill. He called the kid, Tony, over and asked him about Patrice. He claimed he didn't see her.

"We've got to find her; she's only nineteen months old. She can't even say her name so people understand it."

"That young, she couldn't get far," said Tony.

Tony opened the outside door and walked out into the tiny parking lot. Bill and I looked behind the one checkout station and behind the candy display.

We met again near the door. "It's unlikely she got out of the store," said Bill. "She'd have to walk by me and I didn't see her."

"She's not in the parking lot," said Tony. "And I didn't see her walking down the street."

"She didn't go away by herself," I said. "Maybe someone took her. Lots of things can happen to a kid that small." I must have been looking a little manic, because both Tony and Bill were staring at me.

"Calm down," said Bill. "Where did you last see her?"

"Over by the cooler," I said. "She was in the little car. I looked down at my list, and she was gone."

"Let's start there, again," said Tony.

He looked about seventeen, what did he know about looking for kids? But I didn't have a better idea, so I followed him, muttering about calling the police if we didn't find her in the next five minutes.

We got back to the car and cart, right where I left it. Patrice was sitting in the car, eating a green lollipop. I went over and took the lollipop out of her hand. She screamed and tried to grab it from me. I picked her up.

"Who gives lollipops to little kids?" I asked. Patrice started to pound her hands on my chest. I handed the pop to Tony and put her in a bear hug. "Don't you know how dangerous that is?"

"The little girl is fine," said Bill, patting her on the back. "She's just upset you took her treat away from her." He picked up a four-pack of chocolate cookies. "Can she have these? You can watch me unwrap them to make sure they're safe."

I nodded. Bill unwrapped the cookies and gave one to me. I let Patrice go; she took the cookies, and stopped crying and struggling. I looked at her face and realized I was trembling. We were both shaking.

"Are we good now?" asked Bill.

"No," I said. "I want to know where she was and who gave her the pop. Little kids shouldn't be left alone. If somebody saw her, they should have reported it."

A boy with dark hair and eyes, about twelve years old, came to stand next to Bill. Bill mussed his hair and asked him, "When did you get here?"

"Just got home from school. Only a half day today," said the boy.

Bill introduced the child as his son, Billy. The boy walked up to Patrice and called her by name.

"You know Patrice?" I asked.

"Yeah, Mrs. L. comes in with her sometimes," said Billy. "Where's her lollipop?"

"Lollipop?" I looked at the pop, still in Tony's hand. "That lollipop?"

"Yeah, her lollipop," said Billy. "When I came in, she was by the door, so I gave her the pop and brought her back to the car. She likes to ride in the car."

"You gave her the pop?" I asked. Guess I was little loud, as several customers looked at me and Billy took a step backward.

"Yeah, I didn't think she should be hanging out by the door," Billy said.

"Maybe you should keep a closer eye on her, in the future," said Tony.

I gathered up Patrice, put her in the stroller, and left the store before I said something I'd really regret. Now I'll have to explain to Freya why I didn't get any of the things on my list.

CHAPTER THREE

GABE

I DIDN'T SEE THE COP IN THE YARD UNTIL I WAS STANDING in the driveway. Patrice was asleep in the stroller, and I was still fuming about the kid giving her a lollipop. I'd have to watch her more closely from now on.

The cop was looking over my old car. We try not to use it much because gas is expensive; that's why we walked to the store.

"Can I help you?" I asked the cop.

His head came up. He looked toward the front porch. Another cop was standing there, his hand raised to knock on the door. The cop in the driveway was young and skinny and the one on the porch was old and round.

The one in the driveway spoke first. "Jesus Gabriel Leary?" He said Jesus like an Anglo.

It must be serious; they used my full name. My Catholic mother, from Nicaragua, named me after Our Lord and Savior and the archangel that told Mary she was pregnant. My mother never did anything halfway.

"Call me Gabe," I said.

"Mr. Leary." This from the old cop on the porch. "May we come in and talk to you?"

"Is there a problem?" I asked. "Is Charity okay? Is somebody injured?" I looked down at Patrice in the stroller. Despite our adventures this morning, I knew where she was.

"No, Mr. Leary." The officer adjusted his gun belt. "We just have some questions about Stella. May we come in?"

I went to the door and unlocked it. Freya was standing on the other side.

"Who's at the door, hon?" She looked around me and saw the uniforms. "Oh."

I picked up Patrice, stroller and all, and put her into the hallway. My shoulder felt like it was on fire. I'm out on workers' comp because of the shoulder injury.

"I'm Sergeant Barstow," said the older one. "And this is Officer Gates." He gestured toward his partner. "We have some questions about your daughter, Stella."

"Stella's dead," I said. Though, if they'd been looking me up, they knew that.

"Come in and sit down." Freya checked on Patrice in the stroller and left her asleep in the hall. "Have a seat." She waved toward the living room.

After some moving of furniture and questions about coffee (not interested), we all sat in the living room. Officer Gates put a tablet on his knees. Didn't remember seeing it before, but I was a bit distracted. I think I liked the officers with the little pads of paper better. We stared at each other for a few moments.

"Stella died in a car crash," I said.

He made the usual insincere comments. I got tired of hearing "I'm sorry for your loss," but I couldn't think of anything else I'd want people to say to me. I said "thank you," like Freya told me to.

"Where was your daughter driving to?" asked the sergeant.

I felt Freya take my hand. We'd been through this many times, but it hurt every time.

"Stella isn't our daughter, she's our granddaughter," I said. "Her mother, Jade, is our daughter."

"Jade Vega?" This from Gates.

Barstow gave him a dirty look. Guess there was some tension there. I didn't answer. I didn't want to get into a discussion about our daughter and especially not a discussion about her husband, Carlos Vega.

"Yes," Freya said. "Jade's been missing for about a year."

"Missing?' asked Gates. "Did you file a missing person report?"

Freya looked uncomfortable. I told her never to volunteer information, but sometimes she couldn't help herself.

"No," she said. "She just took off. She's an adult, can go where she wants."

Gates looked down at his tablet.

"Where was Stella driving to when she got in the accident?" Barstow repeated his earlier question.

"She worked at the donut shop," I said. "They only do breakfast and lunch, so she was on her way home."

"About 3:00 p.m.?" Barstow didn't consult any notes, he knew this information.

"Yeah, a snowstorm was coming in, so it was already getting dark," said Freya. "She lost control and went off the road."

"There was nothing wrong with the car," I said. "I'd just worked on it the day before and it was running fine."

"You worked on the car?" Barstow leaned forward.

"Yeah, I bought the El Camino new in 1994 and I've done all the work on it." Suddenly I realized what I was saying. "Was something wrong with the car?" If it was my fault that Stella was dead, I'd never forgive myself.

"Some new information has come to light," said Barstow. "Was your granddaughter depressed or upset that day?"

"Stella was fine. Just like every other day." This from Freya.

"She was twenty-four years old, working in a donut shop and raising a five-year-old. She had to drop out of college to take care of the kid." Barstow consulted his notes. "Other people at the donut shop say she didn't have much of a social life?"

"She did okay," I said. "She lived with us; we watched Charity, her daughter, while she worked. She chose to adopt Charity."

"What's that about?" asked Gates. "She adopted her sister's child? But they live with you?"

"Stella's twin, Celeste, has learning disabilities and a hard time coping," said Freya. "We discussed it as a family and decided that Stella should adopt her daughter. We'd help, but Stella was more likely to be able to raise Charity."

"Did Celeste resent her sister?"

I didn't know how to answer that, so I didn't.

"Did Stella have any enemies? Ex-boyfriends or other people who didn't like her?" asked Barstow.

"No, of course not," I said. Alarm bells went off in the back of my head. "Was Stella's death not an accident?"

Barstow looked around the room, not answering my question. He'd earlier seemed interested that I'd worked on her car. "Was there something wrong with the car?" I asked.

"It appears that the brake line was tampered with," Barstow said.

"Tampered with?" I stood up. "It was fine when I worked on it." Freya took my hand and pulled me back into the chair. "The brake line is steel; it doesn't just bend or break."

"We know, Mr. Leary." Barstow adjusted his gun belt. "But there was a leak in the line. The crash was deemed an accident, so nobody looked at the car for several weeks. Somebody just got around to it and found the hole."

"Caused by the accident?" I asked. I hoped.

"No, it appears that someone cut the line." This from Gates. Barstow looked at him and frowned. Guess he didn't like Gates stepping on his lines.

"But it might have been from the accident," said Freya. I could feel her fingers digging into my arm.

"No, ma'am," said Barstow, now back in control. "It was cut. Forensics says it was severed by a metal object, not a stone or the pavement."

Some more moments of silence.

Barstow looked at Gates. I guess that was a signal that he could talk, because he said, "Mr. and Mrs. Leary, where were you on the day Stella died?"

"We were here," said Freya. "Until Stella got home, we had her daughter."

"Wait a minute." I had to interrupt. "Are we suspects?"

"We're just being thorough." Barstow turned his attention to Freya. "Were you both here all evening?"

"Yes." Freya took a tissue out of her pocket. "We were here with Charity until the police arrived to tell us that Stella was at the hospital."

"Are we suspects?" I repeated.

"Did you have any reason to want Stella dead?" asked Barstow.

It took me a few moments to say no.

Gates looked like he wanted back in the conversation. "Do you know of anybody that would want Stella dead?

Both Freya and I shook our heads. I was having difficulties getting my head around the fact that Stella's death might not be an accident.

Barstow asked the question a different way. "Is there anybody that benefits from Stella's death?"

"Just Banks." Freya had a way of getting to the point.

"Who's Banks?" If Barstow was investigating Stella's death, it was likely he knew about Banks. Maybe he was fishing for more information.

I squeezed Freya's hand.

"George Banks is Charity's biological father." Freya seemed determined to get the information out.

"And were George Banks and your daughter married?" asked Barstow.

"Charity is the child of George Banks and our granddaughter, Celeste. Stella adopted her when Celeste couldn't take care of her," Freya explained. "Now Stella is dead, Banks wants custody."

"I see."

It was apparent to me that Barstow already knew this information. If only Freya would stop giving him cause to ask more questions.

"Banks has petitioned to get out of jail," said Barstow.

CHAPTER FOUR

GABE

I HEARD A KNOCK ON THE DOOR. I NEEDED A MINUTE TO digest the information about Banks trying to get out of jail, so I excused myself and went to look out the side window. Bonnie, Charity's speech therapist, stood on the porch. Once you get involved with the social services, somebody is always showing up at your door, wanting to know something or do something. I opened the door.

The knocking woke up Patrice, still in her stroller. She started whining and squirming. Great, now I had cops in the house, a social worker at the door, and a cranky kid. I picked up Patrice and tried to quiet her. She laid her head on my shoulder, put her thumb in her mouth, and looked around.

Freya came out of the living room with both cops. She stopped short when she saw Bonnie. "The officers were just leaving," she said.

"I have some questions," I said.

"Maybe another time," said Officer Barstow. "We have another call."

They strutted to the door, opened it, and left. I closed it after them.

"What was that about?" asked Bonnie. "Why are the police here?"

"They had some more questions about Stella," said Freya. "The investigation is still open."

I didn't want this to go any further. "Did I forget an appointment with you?" I asked. "Charity is at preschool today."

"I know," said Bonnie. "I want to talk to you about something else. Can I come in?"

"Looks like you are," I said. I went to the door and made sure it was shut. Sometimes it sticks. I like Bonnie, even if she is part of social services. She takes a lot of care about her hair. Today it was braided and wrapped around her head. "What's going on?"

I still held Patrice and led the way back to the living room. Bonnie and Freya followed.

"Would you like something to drink?" Freya asked. "I just made coffee."

"No, thanks," said Bonnie. "I won't be staying long."

"Do you want to sit down?" This from Freya, always polite.

I just wanted everybody to leave us alone.

"No, this will only take a minute." Bonnie took a card out of her purse and put it on the table. "This card is from Richard Paoletti, of the local Citizen Advocacy organization. We talked about him a few weeks ago. He can hook you up with a community volunteer who can help you."

"Help us how?" We have so much help now I don't have time to breathe.

"They can pair you with somebody in the community who can help you with Charity and Patrice and make sure Celeste gets the help she needs."

I picked up the card. It originally said "Richard Paoletti, Citizen Advocacy" with an address and phone number. The "Paoletti" was crossed out and "Fontaine" was written in blue ink.

"Why'd he change his name?" I asked.

Bonnie looked confused for a moment, so I showed her the card.

"Oh, Richard recently had some turmoil in his life. He was adopted and found his birth sister, so he decided to take his birth name. It's a long story, but it means that Richard knows about adoption and how it affects a family."

I put the card in my pocket. "Even if he knows about adoption, how is another person in our life going to help? We can barely keep up with the appointments we have now."

"This person will work with you and Freya." Bonnie hitched her purse up on her shoulder. "He or she'll be on your side, to help with getting Stella's social security for Charity and to help you get custody of Patrice. I hear that George Banks, Charity's father, also wants a custody hearing. Probably can help with that, too."

Those were things we could use, and I needed to get to work. "Okay," I said, glancing at Freya. "We'll talk about it."

Now I was late for work. Granted, my boss is my son-in-law, Carlos Vega, but it doesn't look good. I gathered up my wallet, my messenger bag, and a few other things I needed. You can't afford to support a family these days on what's in a workers' comp check. So, like lots of other disabled people, I have a part-time job that I don't tell the workers' comp people about. I

went out to my old car, still parked in the driveway. One day it's not going to start, making me even later than usual. But not today.

Made a few stops on my way to Carlos's cobbler shop, picking up work that needs to be done and a few other things. Pickup and delivery are included in the price of the work; rich people are used to paying for that also.

I hit the hole in the corner of the parking lot. Most of the lot was full, so I parked in the back. Knew the asphalt had worn but the front wheel went into it anyway. Got to remember to pay attention when I drive.

Only my grandson, Chris, sat in the shop when I arrived. His Siberian husky, Alaska, was asleep at his feet. A pile of shoes and shoeboxes was by the door. Same shoes had been there since the shop opened. At first, the shoes stayed there to make the place look busy. Now it was actually busy, nobody had time to move them.

"Hi, Grandpa. How are you doing?" Chris was sitting behind the Formica counter with a tablet on his knees. He worked here too.

"Okay. Had the police people at the house today."

His head came up. "What'd they want?"

"Had some questions about your sister's death. Asked about who worked on the car. Asked about your sister and where she went."

"Did you tell them I worked on the car?"

"I told them I'd always worked on the car. Don't remember whether I told them you helped me."

"Don't tell them. Please."

"Why not?"

Chris looked around the shop. "Because I was supposed to be in school that day. Don't want Dad to know I skipped."

"We worked on the car during school break. You weren't missing anything that day.

Do you skip school often?"

Chris shrugged his shoulders. His father walked in just then, so I didn't ask any more questions.

"You still here?" Carlos said to me. "I thought you had deliveries to make."

"On my way now." I picked the leather bag off the counter and let myself out the back door.

The stops at the veterinarian and the bakery were uneventful. Carlos did good custom work, and people were willing to pay top dollar for it. I set out for the country club on the outskirts of Meredith, the town where I lived. Not that I could afford the fees to join. It was a nice drive down a tree-lined street, classic New England.

The parking attendant knew me and waved me through. The lot was half full and there were no holes. No asphalt either; the parking lot was covered in white pieces of something. Somebody told me it was crushed oyster shells; nearest ocean is over thirty miles away. My bag was lighter after my first stops and didn't hurt my shoulder. I hurried across the parking lot; I had a half dozen more stops to make before the end of the day.

"Hey, Pops!" Somebody was always hailing me at the country

club, telling me I didn't belong and couldn't park my car there. But the managers and I had an understanding.

"Leary, I'm talking to you."

Celeste stood in front of me, looking decades older than the last time I saw her. She had burns on her face and arms and her teeth and skin were gray. She wore a long, patched skirt and a shawl around her shoulders.

"What are you doing here?" Not a great conversation starter, but it was the only thing I could think of. She looked around, as if surprised to realize where she was.

Long pause. "Came to find you."

"Why?" Another long pause. I waited. No questions about her daughters, just a blank stare.

"Can I borrow fifty dollars?" Celeste drew her foot over the bits of the parking lot. "For food." She looked up at the trees. "For Patrice and Charity."

"They're with us. By the way, they're doing fine."

"Larry misses them." Larry was Celeste's no-account boyfriend.

"You back with him?"

"For a while. Got to have a place to live."

"You could go to rehab."

"Ah, Pops, I don't need rehab for slow learning." Celeste scratched the back of her hand.

Both of her hands were red and a blister was filled with liquid at her wrist. No signs of infection, but they didn't look like they'd been cared for, either.

"You still working for Carlos?" she asked. "Still delivering paper bags with money in them?"

"Yeah, and I'm late. Got to get out of here before the dinner rush starts."

"How about you give me a hundred bucks and I don't tell the disability people that you're working?" Celeste pulled the shawl around her shoulders.

I grabbed her hand. "That burn looks bad, it could get infected. You should see a doctor."

"Forgot to turn in the papers for MassHealth. I got no insurance. Can I have some money to go to the urgent care clinic?"

"Wait for me. After I make this delivery, I'll take you to the clinic and I'll pay for it."

"And give me some money?"

I walked away. Didn't want to get into that argument.

She grabbed my arm. "Answer my question. Or maybe I'll go to the cops with what I know."

Other people in the parking lot were looking at us. Not a good scene. I needed to make my deliveries and go.

"We'll talk about this later. You want to get us both arrested? I think I'll do better than you will in jail."

She let go of my arm. "Which car is yours? I'll wait there."

"No. I don't want you in my car when I'm not around." I pointed out my locked car. "Just lean against the bumper, don't make no trouble, and I'll be right back."

I walked around back and entered the clubhouse through the kitchen. I looked more like the help than a member anyway. Antonio, the chef, looked up when I entered.

"You're late."

I looked at my watch. "Right on time."

"Okay, but try to be earlier next time. We're starting dinner prep."

Didn't think he'd care about my day, so I didn't respond. I followed him into his office. His office used to be the storage closet and still had piles of napkins, knives, and industrial-size cans of mustard, relish, tomatoes, and other things I couldn't identify. His desk was jammed up against the back wall and he pulled open its only drawer.

"I've got your boots here." I put them on the table.

"That's four hundred, right?" Antonio laid out four hundred-dollar bills.

"That covers the boots," I said. "You still owe Carlos forty-five hundred. Maybe you'll do better in March Madness, but I can't take any more bets until you pay it off."

"Thought it was four thousand," said Antonio.

"That was last week. Carlos has got business expenses."

"What was that in the parking lot?" Antonio made like he was looking out the window that wasn't in his office.

"Family stuff."

"Seems like you got a lot of family stuff." Antonio stared over my head. "If you make a scene here, we're both screwed. Any complaints, you'll be barred from the premises."

Antonio spoke English with an unidentified accent, but he used words like "barred from the premises."

"Still need the forty-five hundred," I said.

Antonio looked me up and down. I get that a lot, customers trying to see if I'm serious.

"I haven't got the full amount," said Antonio. He laid out six more hundred-dollar bills. "Here's some good faith money."

I picked up the money and put it in my bag.

"We good?" asked Antonio.

"I don't do enforcement. I just report to Carlos what you've paid." I turned and opened the door.

"And keep that family stuff out of here," said Antonio.

I figured he already had enough problems, so I didn't answer.

Celeste was leaning against the car when I got back to the parking lot. She was arguing with the valet. Loudly.

"Lady, you can't be here if you're not a member." The parking attendant, dressed in a red vest, was waving his arms. "You've got to leave."

Celeste leaned back against the car. I hurried over.

"I'll take care of this. She's with me." The parking attendant didn't look happy but the two hundred I gave him every month allowed me to park here when I wanted. "C'mon, Celeste, let's go." I grabbed her arm and put her into the passenger seat. "Don't touch anything." I hurried around the car, passing a twenty to the valet when I went by.

I keep my car clean, but Celeste looked around like it was infected. "Why you still driving this old car?" she asked.

I looked at the cracks in the vinyl dashboard and the duct tape where I'd fixed the seat. "'Cause it's all I can afford," I said. "It gets me where I'm going."

We drove away. Celeste rolled down the window, even though it was March and I had the heat on.

"I'm hungry." Celeste looked at me.

Strange words from a meth addict. She was rubbing her arms and looking around. Withdrawal, or had she taken something while I was inside? Either way, I could do food.

We pulled around to a drive-thru and ordered chicken sandwiches with fries. Sat in the parking lot and ate them. Celeste had ordered barbeque sauce and was dipping her fries in that. We ate in silence for a few minutes.

"So, what are you going to do now?" She was my granddaughter and I was interested in her welfare.

"Maybe I should go to the clinic. This burn hurts."

"Pain meds would be nice too, huh?" I knew her motives well by now.

"You taking me or what?"

"Yeah, I'll take you. What you going to tell them? Your boyfriend was cooking meth and you didn't move fast enough?"

Celeste looked at me through her narrowed eyes.

"Tell them it's a grease fire," she said. "Burned my arms trying to put it out."

"Think they'll believe you?"

"Doesn't matter. Urgent care won't ask too many questions. Just patch me up, give me pills, and refer me to my own doctor. I'll give them the name of some random doctor; they'll try to follow up but will only call a coupla times."

This was a long speech for Celeste. It broke my heart that she knew how to game the system and didn't seem to care.

"But I'll need money for urgent care. My health insurance…"

"I heard you the first time. Why didn't you renew your Mass-Health when you were supposed to?"

"We moved, stuff went to the wrong address, I forgot. You know how it is."

Yeah, I know how it is. She got oxy from clinics when she could, bought stuff on the street or made her own meth when she couldn't. She stayed with her new boyfriend because his brain still functioned enough to remember the basic chemistry.

"You delivering for Carlos?" she asked.

I guess we were finished discussing her health.

"Yeah, I've got a few more stops to make."

"How's Christopher?" Didn't ask about her children, but wanted to know about her brother.

"He's doing good. Working with his dad today." Hell, with it. "Your daughters, Patrice and Charity, are doing good, too."

"Why you say it like that? I know they're my daughters. And I know they're doing good with you and Gram."

"The police showed up today."

"They tried to call me too. I didn't return the call."

We pulled up in front of urgent care.

Celeste turned to me. "Hundred dollars should do it." She stuck out her hand.

"Think I'm giving you a hundred dollars? No way. I'm coming in with you and paying as you go. At the pharmacy too."

Celeste crossed her arms over her chest, rounded her shoulders, and stared at the floor. I have been going to the parents' group at NA and AA for ten years. The act didn't work on me. I got out of the car and walked around to the passenger door. Yanking it open, I took her arm and pulled her out of the car.

"Can't do anything about your habit. But I can make sure you don't get an infection from the burn." Learned that in thirty-eight years at the factory. Saw all kinds of burns and the biggest problem is infection. "Make sure you get antibiotics along with your pain meds."

She dragged her feet some but came along with me. The clinic closes at 8:00 p.m. and it was already 7:35 p.m. Receptionist didn't look warm and inviting.

I stepped up to the desk. Celeste stood behind me, arms still crossed and head down.

"We'd like to see a doctor, please."

The receptionist looked up, slid a paper across the desk. "What's the problem?"

"She got burned. Bad."

Receptionist looked around me to Celeste. "Could I have your insurance information, please?"

I stepped in front of Celeste. "No insurance. I'll pay cash."

The receptionist looked up and recited what sounded like a speech. "Most Massachusetts residents are entitled to health insurance. And there are penalties for not having it. Would you like an insurance application form?"

"Not now. Just want to get her seen." I knew about the application form. You filled it out, got copies of every document you needed, called the helpline and waited on the phone for hours until somebody answered. Used up all your minutes being passed from person to person and then ended up with no minutes on your phone and no health insurance. "I'll deal with the health insurance later."

I took the form she handed to me and we sat down. It was 8:20 p.m. before we saw the doctor and we were out of there by 8:35 p.m. I drove Celeste to the pharmacy and made sure she filled the antibiotic, burn cream, and pain medications. Not that I could make her take them. We walked out to the car and she kept on walking, right past me and out of the parking lot. No "thank you" or anything.

I didn't finish my deliveries that night. It was a good thing, because I used some of Carlos's money to pay for the clinic. Figured Celeste was his stepdaughter, he ought to foot the bill. Hope he saw it that way.

WEDNESDAY

MARCH 11, 2020

CHAPTER FIVE

GABE

I WOKE THE NEXT MORNING TO THE SMELL OF BACON AND eggs. And it wasn't even Sunday. I got dressed because I wanted to finish my deliveries and talk to Carlos before we went to the cemetery. Like I do every morning, I walked through the house to check things out. It doesn't take long; our house is small. A living room and eat-in kitchen downstairs. There's a room in the back that was a playroom when the kids were little. It's full of junk now. Three bedrooms upstairs. Our big bedroom in the front and two smaller rooms in back. One bathroom upstairs and a half bath down.

When I walked into the kitchen, I saw Celeste holding Patrice. Didn't know whether to object to her being there or to encourage her to visit her daughter. Freya was going back and forth from the stove to the table and she put a plate down in front of Patrice and Celeste. The hand that reached for bacon was wrapped in clean bandages and covered with gold bracelets. She'd changed her dress too. This one was blue; not new, but cleaner than the one she had on yesterday.

"Morning Celeste, Patrice, Freya." I sat down at the table. "How are you doing?"

"Hand's doing better. No infection." Celeste gave Patrice a spoon and they both dug into the scrambled eggs.

"I'm glad you're here." I sat down. "Where's Charity?"

"She's still asleep." Freya put my breakfast in front of me.

Patrice dropped egg onto Celeste's dress.

"You can put her in the high chair. Don't want to ruin your dress." Freya dabbed at the egg with a towel.

"No," said Celeste. "I want to hold my daughter."

Freya sat down at the table. I didn't notice the purple stones laying there before she started playing with them.

Freya had laid out three runes on the table. I put my hand on them.

She took the runes off the table and put them into their bag. "Change is coming."

I'd lived with her long enough to not ignore her readings. "Good change or bad change?"

"Don't know. But what we've been dealing with is going to change."

"Does that mean we won't have to raise kids anymore?" The minute the words left my mouth I wanted to take them back. Freya's life was raising her grandkids. I loved them too but it would be nice, for once, to travel somewhere without dragging diaper bags, toys, and all the other stuff that comes with entertaining kids. "I'm sorry, I didn't mean that."

"I know you don't mean it. But it would be nice to be the grand-parents for a change."

Freya got up to get another cup of coffee and came back and put one in front of Celeste too. "So, Celeste, are you going to the ceme-tery with us? It's been three weeks since Stella died."

As if any of us could forget how long Stella had been gone.

Celeste got real interested in playing with the Cheerios in front of Patrice. Moved three or four of them around in a pattern before she answered. "Maybe. But I came back for my portfolio."

Celeste had trained as a graphic artist; her portfolio consisted of half a dozen unfinished posters and drawings.

"You got a job?" I asked.

"Just looking." She put Patrice in the high chair and put out a few more Cheerios. "Thought I would get my portfolio and see what was out there.

"Maybe that's the change in the runes. A new job for you."

Celeste stared at her grandmother. "Don't think so."

Patrice started banging on the tray of her high chair. It was an old high chair—originally used for Freya—and made of metal, so it made quite a clanging noise. Celeste pushed more Cheerios her way. With a loud no, Patrice swept everything on the tray—the Cheerios, the bowl with the scrambled eggs, and the spoon—to the floor. Freya and I stood up at the same time and bumped our heads together. Celeste leaned down to pick up the items on the floor and Freya went to the sink, soaked a towel, and put it over her eye.

This is how the people from the court found us. Freya putting cold water on her eye, me holding my head, and Celeste on the floor. Two of them this time. Not only did everybody think they had a right to drop in to our house, they brought a friend. An older woman and a short, dark man. They stood on the back porch, looking through the window in the door. Not sure how much they saw.

I opened the back door and stepped onto the tiny back porch.

"May we come in?" asked the dark-haired man. His hair was braided in short rows and he held a clipboard with papers on it. Dark polo shirt and khakis. The woman was several inches taller and about fifty pounds lighter. She was dressed in a light blue dress with blue shoes on her feet. Shoes that had ribbons wrapped around the tops, up over her ankles. Didn't look like she spent much time around children, who tend to mess up an outfit like that.

"No," I responded. "Not a good time now." Tiny porch, more like a landing, hardly held three of us. I shut the inner door and the storm door behind me. "I've got to go to work, and the children just woke up."

"Aren't you going to invite us in?" This from the woman. "I'm Mary Allen; I represent Charity in her court case."

I'd been through this before, knew my rights. "You were sup-posed to be here yesterday. Now's not a good time. If you want to talk to us, call to make another appointment or we'll come to the office. Bringing birth certificates, Mass Health cards, whatever you want." I didn't want her to report to the court that I was "uncoop-erative"; I've been called that before. "Charity's asleep now, so it's best you come back later."

Ms. Allen backed off the porch and onto the step. She smoothed the front of her dress. Guess we were too grubby for her.

"We'll come back tomorrow." The man switched the clipboard from one hand to the other and held out his right hand. "Forgot to introduce myself. I'm Dwayne Bigelow. I'm Attorney Allen's assistant."

I ignored the hand and, after a few seconds, he dropped it down by his side. Guess Attorney Allen was afraid to see us alone.

"I'm Gabe Leary. This is my house. Please go." I opened both doors, stepped inside, and deliberately locked both doors behind me.

Celeste was at the sink, putting some ice cubes into the towel Freya had wet before. She wrapped the towel around the ice cubes and put it to her mother's eye. "Thought you were going to work," said Celeste.

"You all right?" Dumb question, of course she wasn't all right. "I just wanted to check on you before I left."

"Yeah." Dumb answer. "Thought I'd put the ice on to make sure the eye didn't swell. Might get written up for domestic violence. Then they'll ask me all the questions about whether anybody is hurt-ing me."

Just being cautious. When Celeste was small, she got some bruises we couldn't explain and didn't remember how she got them. We were hassled by the DCF people and the police for months before they decided we didn't beat her.

Freya and Celeste sat back down to finish their interrupted

breakfast. My eggs were cold and the bacon was sitting in a pile of grease. Kind of lost my appetite.

"Give Patrice some Cheerios." I motioned to the high chair.

"She'll just throw them around again." Celeste put another handful into her mouth. "Okay, just a few." She lined up four of them on the tray.

Patrice picked one up and studied both sides of it.

"I've got to go," I said. "Didn't finish my deliveries yesterday."

"That was my fault," said Celeste. "And I didn't say thank you."

"How is your hand?" I asked. "Did the cream and medicine help?"

Celeste patted the bandages. "It's still a little sensitive, but doing much better."

"Did you think any more about rehab?"

"I don't need rehab." Celeste moved the Cheerios around on Patrice's tray. "I'll just stop."

I wanted to say something else but Freya shook her head. I left.

The two late deliveries went smoothly. Both the clerk in the town hall and the janitor at the school had lost some money, so they weren't anxious to see me anyway. But both paid up. I was still short the $315 I'd spent on Celeste at the clinic.

Carlos leaned on the counter but looked up when I entered. He nodded at me but said nothing.

I put my bag on the counter and set out the money I collected, still divided by the person who gave it to me.

"You're late with the money," said Carlos. He picked up one of the packets and started counting it.

I waited, without comment, while he counted all the money.

"You're short," he said, as he placed the money under the counter.

I studied the pattern in the counter. Gray and black, it didn't take long. "I spent three hundred fifteen at the clinic," I said. "On Celeste, your stepdaughter." Like he wouldn't know who Celeste was.

"You owe me for that." Carlos took out his tablet where he kept his accounts. "I'm talking about the forty-five hundred from Antonio. You didn't get that."

I'd forgotten about Antonio. "He only wanted to give me the four hundred bucks for the boots," I said. "I got another six hundred out of him."

"Leaving him short," said Carlos.

The door banged shut.

"I told you to be careful with the door." Carlos spoke over my shoulder.

Chris came and leaned on the counter, with the same slouch as his father. "Oh, good, Grandpa's still here." His dog, Alaska, sniffed around at the shoes and leather piled on the floor.

Chris usually ignored me, or answered questions in grunts.

"You're looking for me?"

"Yeah." Chris took a piece of paper out of the pocket of his jacket. "I want to go to the cemetery with you today."

This was a day for surprises. I'd gone to Stella's grave every week, but I don't remember Chris going since his sister died.

"Can I go?" he asked.

"It's fine with me, if it's okay with your dad. Isn't today a school day?"

Carlos shrugged.

"Great, I've got to get some things from the back, and then we can leave. Dad, please feed Alaska if I'm not back in time." Chris disappeared through the back door, into the office. Alaska followed him, still sniffing at random items.

"Take good care of my kid." Carlos tapped his finger on my chest. "And you still owe me for the money you didn't collect. I'll get it from you later."

With that warning, Carlos followed his son into the office.

CHAPTER SIX

GABE

Chris and I returned to my house to pick up the others. Freya, Celeste, and Patrice were still sitting at the kitchen table. Charity gnawed on a piece of toast, still in her pajamas.

"Hey, little bro," Celeste greeted Chris. "What are you doing here?"

Chris's head was down, looking at his phone. "Thought I'd go to the cemetery with the grands."

Celeste looked at Freya, then at me. "Maybe I'll go with you too," she said.

"We can all go," said Charity. "After breakfast." She continued to eat her toast.

This was a day for surprises, but I was still confused. "Okay. Why do you want to go to the cemetery with us?"

Celeste shook the bracelets on her arm. "I want to go to Stella's grave."

"Why?" None of my grandchildren shared my interest in visiting Stella and all of them had made that quite plain.

"Haven't been there before. Thought you and me and Gram could go. Charity and Patrice too."

At the mention of her name, Patrice reached for one of Celeste's bracelets. "Pretty," she said.

"What's going on with you?" Sometimes there's nothing like the direct approach. "You're acting strange."

"Can't I miss my family? Can't I come home to visit?" Celeste removed her bracelets from Patrice's hand.

Freya stepped between us. "Leave her alone, Gabe. If she wants to go to the cemetery, then let's go. Chris and the girls, too."

"Did you put them up to this?" I asked Freya.

"Not me," she said. After forty years of marriage, I can usually tell when she's lying. She seemed as surprised as me.

We left for the cemetery. Of course, it wasn't that fast or easy. Had to pack a diaper bag for Patrice and get her changed because her clothes were covered with her breakfast. Then Charity wanted some of Patrice's Cheerios, so we put them into a bag for her. Celeste had to do some female thing with her clothes and hair and Chris kept digging through the pockets of his jacket. It was past noon by the time we got to the cemetery. Freya sat in the grass and fed Charity and Patrice sandwiches from a sack I didn't know she had. I was hungry too—my breakfast had been interrupted—but nobody packed a bag for me.

The cemetery is a nice peaceful one, set back from the road. Had an upper and lower section. Upper had oak trees and the lower was around the pond. Freya and I bought the lot just after Stella died. Argued about whether she would want oak trees or a pond. Freya won; Stella's buried by the pond. With the insurance money, we bought a granite headstone that had just been installed. Freya got her way about the gravesite, but I insisted about the engraving. No flowery phrases, just a statement of who and what she was.

STELLA JADE LEARY
Born November 3, 1996 Died February 21, 2020
Beloved Daughter, Granddaughter, Sister, Mother

I wandered away from the family to my brother's grave. He and his wife were buried near the pond also. Patrick Raphael Leary and his wife, Leslie (Canon) Leary. My brother survived two tours in Vietnam, and died in a car accident in Meredith, Massachusetts.

I watched Chris wander away from the family group. He climbed to the top of the hill and looked over the other side. Then he turned around, looking in each direction for a few minutes. Like he was expecting to be attacked on the top of the hill. Celeste joined him; they spoke for a few minutes, and then separated and walked in opposite directions back to the pond.

Charity joined me by my brother's grave. "Whose grave is this?" she asked.

She asked the same question every time. And I gave her the same answer.

"It's your grandpa and grandma."

"My bio, biocal grandpa and grandma."

"Yes, your biological grandma and grandpa. They died and we adopted Jade, their daughter."

"Jade is my grandma too."

"Yes, she is. It's family, it's complicated."

"I'm adopted too." Charity pulled a blade of grass out of the ground.

That was where we always ended. "Yes, Mama Stella adopted you when Mama Celeste couldn't take care of you."

Charity stared at Celeste. "But Mama Celeste is here and Mama Stella's not."

There was that. So far, Celeste had not asked for increased contact with Charity. She seemed content just to be part of family outings. And then she'd dropped Patrice off for us to raise. My head hurt.

The conversation was cut short when Patrice started crying. She had started walking toward the pond, but Freya stopped her. Not just crying, but one of her all-out tantrums. She screamed for several minutes, until Charity forgot her questions for me. Freya distracted Patrice with her yellow bunny and things got quiet again.

Chris ignored the drama with Patrice and walked back toward

the entrance to the cemetery. A workman, in a green, one-piece uniform, was raking the grass. Seemed a little early for that, as the ground was mostly mud, not grass. Chris went up to him and they spoke for several minutes. The workman gestured toward a green sedan, not very clean, parked up on the hill. Chris left the workman and walked toward the car.

As he was approaching the car from behind, a tall woman with dark hair got out of the passenger side of the vehicle. Chris hesitated for a moment and then approached her.

CHAPTER SEVEN

GABE

CELESTE SAUNTERED DOWN THE ROAD TO WHERE I WAS standing. "Do you think Stella's in Heaven?" she asked.

I continued to stare at Chris and the unknown woman.

Celeste looked in the same direction. "Who's Chris talking to? Do you know her?"

"No," I said. "But they've been talking for a few minutes."

"I'm going to see what's going on." Celeste started across the graves, toward where Chris and the woman continued their conversation.

"I'll come with you."

Celeste looked back over her shoulder. "I think Gram needs your help with the kids."

I turned around. Patrice was making another break for the pond, this time followed by Charity. Before I could turn back and suggest that Celeste care for her own children, she was striding toward Chris and the car. I went back, helped Freya get the girls settled on the grass, and we played several rounds of patty-cake.

About five minutes later, Celeste and Chris rejoined us.

"What was that about?" asked Freya.

"Nothing," said Celeste.

Chris shrugged. I looked around him to see the car leaving the cemetery.

"What did they want?" Freya is persistent.

"Just wanted directions." Chris looked uncomfortable. "Lots of people died in our family."

"Family's had some hard times," I said. "Enough of this gloom and doom, we need to be getting back home."

Again, this process took a while. Had to gather up Charity and Patrice and the remains of her lunch. Bread scraps were fed to the ducks in the pond and everything else was picked up and put back into the car. We strapped the girls into their car seats. Chris got in the car and pulled out his phone, tapping away at it.

We drove home. Chris decided he wanted to stay for supper and texted his dad, who agreed. Meal times are noisy at our house. Even when it's just Freya, Charity, Patrice, and me, there are pots and pans dragged out and filled, Patrice banging on her high chair, and trying to tie up the ends of the day. With Chris trying to help, it was chaos. But my efficient wife can cook in a hurricane. And did during Hurricane Sandy, on the gas stove, with no electricity and with the winds whistling around us. We had a pound of hamburger and she added pasta and canned tomatoes and stretched it, just like she did back then.

I just sat at the table and looked around at my family. Freya is taller than me and blond and blue-eyed, as fits her Viking heritage. Her name before our marriage was Olafsonn and she said her grandmother taught her about casting and reading runes. Celeste had the straight, black hair from her mother. Chris's was thicker and wavy, the influence of Carlos and his Puerto Rican ancestors. And, of course, me, with my Nicaraguan mother and Irish father. Charity and Patrice were still under construction.

"Don't forget we're going to see the lawyer tonight." Freya continued to stir the food on the stove as she turned to me.

"I haven't forgot," I said. Though I had. "Six thirty, isn't it?"

"Seven." Freya tasted the concoction she was making. "Only time you weren't working and she wasn't in court."

"What does she need to talk about?"

"Court on Friday. I have some papers to give her."

I knew the papers were about Celeste and her floating in and out of our lives, but I didn't want to discuss it with her present.

A knock at the door. I wasn't expecting anyone else and didn't feel in the mood for company. Chris jumped up and answered it before I could stop him. A murmured conversation took place in the hallway. I got up to stop anybody else from coming into the house.

Chris was in the hallway, hugging a woman. Not a girl, but a woman. If she was a friend of his, I'd have to talk to him. Even from the back, I could see that her top didn't meet her jeans and that the jeans were way too tight. Her hair had orange streaks in it.

Then she turned around and I saw my brother's round face and arched eyebrows. My brother has been dead over forty years. I looked again and realized it was my daughter, Jade. Chris hugged his mother.

"Hi Dad," said Jade. "Are you surprised to see me?"

"Yeah." I was surprised. Good thing she hadn't asked if I was happy to see her.

"Are you going to invite me in?"

She was family. "Of course," I said. I went up to her and gave her a hug.

Chris and I followed her into the kitchen. She sat down at the table as if she had dinner with us every night.

"Look, it's Mom." Chris was almost wetting his pants; hopping from one foot to another like he was four years old, not seventeen.

"Come on in. Sit down." This from my wife, oblivious to the fact that Jade was already sitting. "Tell us how you've been."

I still don't know what I said to her. Jade swung her long, black hair over her shoulder, like she had since she was five years old. She had on a pink top that showed what cleavage she had, jeans, a short jacket and boots. Her only jewelry was green earrings. She looked better than the last time I saw her, almost a year ago.

"Where have you been?" I asked. "And why haven't you contacted us before now?"

Jade hung her head and let her hair cover her face. Like she didn't want to look at us. Freya was having none of it. She came up from her chair, put her hands on both sides of Jade's face, lifted her head, and looked into her eyes.

"I missed you," said my wife.

Jade burst into tears. Jade, who didn't cry when her parents died when she was five years old. Jade, who didn't cry when she came to live with Freya and me, still kids ourselves. Jade, who didn't cry when we took her children to raise as our own. Freya passed her a tissue.

Jade sniffled for a few minutes. Freya declared it was time to eat and started passing out bowls and utensils and getting everybody settled at the table. Bread was passed and drinks were poured. It was quiet for a few minutes as we all concentrated on the food.

When Jade stopped sniffling, Celeste put down her spoon and looked at her mother. "Why didn't you meet us at the cemetery like we planned?" she asked.

Like they planned? Celeste expected Jade and didn't seem ashamed of admitting it.

Jade went over and hugged Celeste. Now they both were crying. "I meant to. But I couldn't get a ride out there. I thought I'd wait here."

"I looked all around for you." Chris almost pouted. "Thought you left us again."

I looked around at my family. Was I the only one that didn't know that Jade planned to come home? As they used to say: who knew what and when did they know it? I felt betrayed and left out, as if everyone threw a party and didn't invite me. I thought I was controlling my anger well when I asked, "Where have you been? And did everybody know you were around but me?"

Jade's hair hung down in front of her face again. Chris looked around the room. Celeste played with her bracelets which made a tinkling, Christmas-like sound. Patrice was asleep, exhausted from the trip to the cemetery. Charity was playing in the corner. Freya went over to the kitchen counter, got out the coffee maker and the coffee and started to put the coffee into the filter. The rich, earthy smell filled the room. Still, nobody talked.

"We just heard yesterday, Grandpa." Chris looked at me and now seemed eager to tell his story. "She called and said she was coming to see us. I was emailing her when you came into the store. To meet her in the cemetery." He got up and took the coffee mugs out of the cupboard. "Gramma didn't know. We wanted it to be a surprise."

I was surprised. And angry. The kids didn't know any better than to keep it a secret. I was relieved that Freya didn't keep the secret from me. Rule in our marriage was that you could not talk about something, but don't lie. Jade coming back meant a huge secret and I was glad she wasn't in on it. All this going through my brain and what I said was, "Where have you been?"

"It's a long story."

Whole family is talking like one of those reality shows. Nobody is saying nothing but I can't believe they all don't have lots of thoughts about Jade and where she went and why she's back. I'm still stuck at what I missed out on in her life. Freya came over to the table with mugs of coffee; Chris followed her with creamer and sugar. Nobody in this family used artificial sweetener. Chris and Stella because they don't need it and me because I don't care. Mugs were passed around and everybody fixed their coffee.

And then Jade started talking. About the twins' father, Robertson, and how he got arrested for some armed robbery. Jade was with him but needed to disappear for a while. The story didn't hang together well, but that was typical of Jade.

"You look good," said Freya.

"I'm straight now. Got new teeth too." Jade smiled, her teeth like Chicklets, all huge and lined up. Better than the originals, which were crooked at the bottom because she didn't get dental care early enough. "I decided it was safe to come home." She took a sip of coffee. "Thought it was. But there was somebody in the cemetery. That's why I didn't meet you there." She didn't seem to realize she told two different stories within the last half hour—one about waiting at the house for us, and one about going to the cemetery and leaving. Jade rummaged through her huge purse. "Bought a gift for Charity and Patrice too." She dragged out a Fisher Price toy telephone. When Jade was a kid, they looked like phones. This one looked like the mobile phones we all carried. "Thought you could teach her how to call me, if she ever wants to."

Jade was good at not talking about things that bothered her. Even when she should. Like the remark about somebody after her. Like I was supposed to forget about it because she gave Patrice a gift she couldn't use for months, and Charity already knew how to make phone calls.

"What do you mean there was somebody in the cemetery?" This from Freya, who was wise to Jade's ways too. "Did somebody follow you there? More important, did somebody follow you here?"

"I think they were waiting for me in the cemetery." Jade moved things around in her bag and pulled out a pack of generic cigarettes. "Don't think they followed me here." She knocked the pack against the table, took out one cigarette, and put it in her mouth.

"What do you mean you don't think they followed you here? Some unknown people coming to the house where your children and grandchildren are." Freya reached over and removed the cigarette from her mouth. "And there's still no smoking in this house."

"I think Chris and I should take the kids to the park," said Celeste. She started packing up Patrice's bottles and diapers.

"But I want to stay here and see my mother." This protest from Chris.

"Later," was Celeste's answer. She gathered up her stuff and Charity and Patrice's stuff and pushed Chris and the carriage out the door.

Leaving me and Freya and Jade alone in the kitchen. I got up to get more coffee. Freya turned off the remains of the supper, still on the stove.

"I read you in the runes," said Freya.

"What did you see? That I was coming home?"

"No, but your stone came up in my daily reading. That hasn't happened in a year."

"Mom, I didn't come back because of that."

I saw my opening. "Why did you come back?"

"I told you. I got sick of living in Arizona and not seeing my family."

"But you said you were followed at the cemetery." I couldn't get past this, that Jade might have brought danger with her. "Are you sure you are safe?"

Jade looked around the kitchen. Like the stains on the front of the dishwasher and the potholders made by the kids were going to change. She picked at the embroidery on the tablecloth. I didn't stop her; we bought the tablecloth at a yard sale.

"You may be over forty, but you made decisions like a fourteen-year-old. You could have put us all in danger. How am I going to protect Charity and Patrice?" Jade had only been home an hour, and I was already exasperated.

"Charity and Patrice? They have a home, and food, and people to protect them. What about me?" Jade burst into tears again.

I can't tell whether Jade's tears are real. They are loud and she gulped air like every breath was her last. And the chances are fifty-fifty that they are real. Freya reached over and took her hand but made no other move to comfort her.

Jade drew in a long breath. "George wants custody of Charity. The judge ordered a new trial."

"I know that," I said. "Took most of the money in Stella's insurance to hire a lawyer to keep Charity with us." I passed Jade a tissue. "But how did you know about it?"

Jade stared into the distance, like she wasn't going to answer me. She often didn't.

"Chris told me," she said.

"When were you talking to Chris?"

"I don't know." Jade blew her nose. "He wanted my help."

"Your help with what?" This from Freya.

More staring by Jade.

Freya came over and sat across from Jade. "Wanted your help with what?"

CHAPTER EIGHT

GABE

JADE TOOK A MOMENT, AS IF THINKING ABOUT HOW TO answer her mother's question.

"Chris wanted me to come home. Said he missed Stella and wanted a mother." Jade seemed sincere. Of course, she'd been play-acting her entire life.

I decided to take this conversation in another direction. "Why come home now?" I asked.

"Charity." Jade drummed her nails on the table. In addition to new teeth, her nails were long and polished. She was trying to make a good impression.

"Charity?" Freya sat back down.

More tapping from Jade. "Yeah, Charity." Tap, tap, tap. "I want custody. Want Carlos and Chris and Charity and me to be a family." Tap, tap, tap. "Cuz I'm clean and can take care of her. And I'm her grandmother."

"Charity's spent her entire life with Stella, and with us during the day. She should stay with people she knows." I had to stop and take a breath. "She doesn't know you."

"Charity knows she's adopted," said Jade. "She knows Celeste is her mother; Celeste can't take care of her, so she went to live with

Stella. Now Stella's gone, I can adopt her. She can still stay with you during the day."

It almost sounded logical, the way she laid it out.

"No." This from Freya. "No, no, no, no." She was waving her hands above her head. "You're not taking my child."

"Didn't say I was taking your child. Just said we might discuss it."

"And where you going to take the child?" Freya asked. "Where you living anyway?"

"I've got a place, over on Beaumont Road," said Jade. "Besides, if I get the kids, maybe I can live with Carlos."

Our conversation was interrupted by the return of the grandkids from the park. Coats and mittens were scattered around the room.

"What's going on?" asked Chris.

"Maybe we could all do something together, tonight," said Jade.

"Your father and I have an appointment." Freya picked up the bowls from the table and put them it the sink. "Chris is staying with the girls for a couple of hours."

"Great, I'll stay too." Jade smiled at Chris. "Maybe we can all watch a movie together."

"It'll have to be some lame kid movies," said Chris. "Girls won't watch anything good."

"We'll figure it out." Jade flashed her too-white teeth at all of us. And that's how we left them, while we went to see the lawyer.

———

The lawyer, Marcy Warner, was recommended to us by the grandparent support group. Her office was on the first floor of an apartment building, next to a beauty parlor. A common entryway led to both offices, and the entire building smelled of something Freya said was peroxide. Marcy had two rooms: a waiting room and her office. The waiting room had flowered wallpaper and a few chairs with cushions and wooden arms. One wall had a fireplace, probably original to the building. Over it hung Marcy's diploma from Suffolk Law School. Once or twice, her assistant was sitting at the desk in the waiting room. Not tonight. We used Stella's insurance to pay for the lawyer and so we did night appointments and ran around and got documents ourselves, to keep the cost down.

Marcy met us at the door and took us into her office. The two rooms probably were one many years ago, so her office was just a square with a window in one side. The same flowered wallpaper, two chairs, and a desk for Marcy. From previous visits, I knew the large closet held a printer and office supplies. Though Marcy had a new, shiny computer on her desk, she sat down, took out a yellow pad, and took notes on that.

"I just wanted to talk to you before court on Friday," she began. "George Banks has filed for custody of Charity." She laid a paper in front of us. "And he's asking for visits."

"I don't want Charity going to the jail to visit her father." Freya's position hadn't changed. "That's not a place for a five-year-old."

"Why does Banks get to ask for custody again, anyway? Didn't we go through this once?" I remembered the first time, Banks's attorney filing motions and dragging things out. Waiting to see if Charity could stay with Stella and stay with us. I didn't want to do it again.

"His attorney filed for a new trial and Judge Hartwell granted the motion. She's just back from maternity leave, maybe she felt for the father." Marcy straightened some already-straight files on her desk.

"Yeah, back a few months, when Celeste filed for more visits, our case was late because they were having a baby shower for the judge," I said. "But that shouldn't affect what she does."

"It shouldn't, but you can never tell." Marcy took some notes on her yellow pad. "Judge Hartwell's pregnancy was a surprise; her other kids are teenagers. Reports are it's made her more receptive to parents."

"But we've had Charity for almost three years. You said it was over. And now we have to do it again because some chemist, not even connected with the case, screwed up." Freya said this in an even tone. She was doing better than me. I wanted to scream.

Marcy looked out the window, as if the answers were there. "This has been a mess for all the attorneys practicing in Massachusetts," she said. "Yes, a chemist at the state lab was using and selling cocaine and other drugs and giving false reports to the court. Thousands of convictions were brought into question. Including George Banks's incarceration."

"But Banks pled guilty," I said. "Doesn't that show he knew it was cocaine, even if the chemist screwed up the test?"

"It's the innocent until proven guilty theory." Marcy shook her head. "Banks doesn't have to prove he's innocent, the Common-wealth has to prove he's guilty. Without the drug test, they can't do that. And all the drug tests were contaminated, because nobody can tell what was tested and what wasn't. So he was released."

"Then he takes a gun and threatens the judge. And his girlfriend, the attorney who brought the gun into the courthouse, threatens my wife." I realized my voice was getting louder. Freya grabbed my hand. "At least he's back in jail again, on the gun charges."

"Attorney Christensen threatened you?" Marcy turned to Freya.

"Not exactly threatened." Freya's need to be precise annoyed me. "She said that Banks would ask for custody of Patrice, too, if we didn't agree to visits with Charity. She said she'd bring up Celeste's drug use and Jade's history, to prove we shouldn't raise any more kids."

"It's unlikely that Banks will get custody," Marcy said.

"That's not the point," said Freya. "I'm scared. Too many things have gone wrong with my grandchildren and great-grandchildren. If Tracy can cause enough confusion, we might not get custody of the children."

I took Freya's hand. I didn't have anything to say, because I know how things can get screwed up with too many people involved. But I wanted her to know I was on her side.

"She doesn't have standing," said Marcy.

I must have looked confused, because she went on.

"In order to bring a lawsuit, a person has to have an interest in the outcome," Marcy continued. "Not just that she wants to be involved, but that there is a legal interest. Tracy has no legal standing, other than the partner of the father. She can't file motions; most likely the judge will not even allow her into the courtroom."

"But she says she can get George to do things, things to slow down everything." I'm fed up with this whole court thing. "Banks says that he's getting out of jail. What will happen then?"

Marcy looked from me, to Freya, and back to me. "Like most people locked up, Banks will say that he will be released, and in a position to care for Charity. But Banks has some serious charges, and he'll have to deal with them first." Marcy took another file from her drawer. "But your daughter, Jade, has filed for custody of both children."

"When did she do that?" I was so surprised I blurted it out. A little loud, I guess, because Marcy pushed back in her chair. "Sorry. It's just that, until today, we didn't even know Jade was around. And she hasn't seen Charity or Patrice for almost a year."

Freya shifted in her chair. "Does she have a chance? For either child?"

"She's got lots of attachments to her motion." Marcy flipped through a dozen pages. "From detox, from her recovery coach, from her doctor, all saying she's sober and doing well." Marcy put the file on her desk. "And she's twenty years younger than you are."

"But the kids don't know her." Freya leaned forward in her chair.

"It may be to your advantage that the matter is in juvenile court." Marcy put out her hand, as if to calm Freya. "Judge Reynolds, in probate and family court, has heard this before. As Banks has filed for custody in juvenile court, most likely Judge Reynolds will do nothing until the other matter involving Charity is resolved."

"What about Patrice? Does that get put on hold too?" Freya asked.

"It might. It's likely," said Marcy. "Judge Reynolds will be reluctant to do anything until the matter of fitness of the parents is resolved."

"We go to court, pay you, and nothing happens?" Not the first time it had happened, but I wanted to be sure.

"Unfortunately, yes." Marcy shook her head. "When you filed for temporary guardianship of Charity, we did it in probate and family court because there was no open case in juvenile court. When Banks was granted a new trial in juvenile court, they took over primary jurisdiction. Nothing will happen until that matter is resolved."

"And how long will that take?" asked Freya. "And why does what happened with his criminal charges mean the custody gets done over?" She finally sounded pissed.

"If you want to go to trial, several years," said Marcy. "If you're willing to settle, give Banks some visitation rights, it could be shorter."

Freya pressed her lips together. "Let us think about it." She rummaged around in her purse and brought out an envelope. "What about Patrice? Can we still get custody of her?"

"Is Banks Patrice's father too?" Marcy asked.

"There's no name on the birth certificate." Freya laid it on the desk, with Patrice's social security card and her MassHealth card. "We have all the papers here."

Marcy picked up the birth certificate. "As there is no named father, we will need to publish for an unknown father. That means we run a legal notice in the newspaper. We can file this in probate court and get you temporary guardianship. I've already done the paperwork; the court just needs this birth certificate to complete the process."

Freya shifted in her seat. "George Banks's girlfriend and sometime lawyer said he might ask for custody of Patrice too. I said I wanted paternity testing. She said he may not need it."

"That depends." Marcy leaned back in her chair. "If he and the mother agree that he is the father, they can sign an Acknowledgement of Paternity without testing. Did your granddaughter say he was the father?"

"She hasn't said anything," I said. "Can't we ask for testing anyway?"

"You don't have standing," Marcy said. "Only the mother and the father can ask for testing."

"But we're the grandparents and we've been raising these kids." I'd thought I could stay calm, but this was ridiculous. "And you haven't answered Freya's question about why the custody should get screwed up because of the chemist."

"The law says only the parents can ask for paternity testing. If they agree that Banks is the father, and sign the necessary documents, he is the father." Marcy aligned the papers on her desk. "As for the custody hearing, Judge Hartwell used a 'but for' test. But for Banks being incarcerated, he might have custody of Charity. Because the incarceration was overturned, he gets another chance. All the tests run by the chemist are suspect, so all the convictions are void."

"What about if Banks is arrested for Stella's death?" I asked.

That stopped Marcy for about three seconds. "Is there a chance of that happening?"

"I don't know," I admitted. "But police came to our house today and they seemed very interested that Banks would benefit from Stella's death. They now think it wasn't an accident."

Marcy recovered quickly. "I'll subpoena the police report and the autopsy." She made a note in the file.

I didn't say anything, for fear I'd say the wrong thing. The next move was up to Celeste, Jade, or Banks.

THURSDAY

MARCH 12, 2020

CHAPTER NINE

JADE

I DIDN'T GET QUITE THE RECEPTION I EXPECTED YESTERDAY. Thought my parents would be more excited to see me, but they think I'm a screwup. Just "Hi, Jade, welcome back," when I spent a year getting myself together, getting my teeth fixed, and getting into a good place with my life. Okay, five months, because the first few months were spent really screwing up. I needed to hit bottom, as they say in the recovery groups. It just took me a little longer than most.

Chris was happy to see me. I have a special place for my youngest, not because he's the only boy, but because he didn't grow up under the influence of my parents. With them, everything had to look good; everybody had to do stuff for family. It's tiring.

I made plans to meet Chris today and spend some time together. He's done a good job keeping the phone I sent him a secret. Even from his father. Maybe I'm so fond of Chris because he's like his father and I've been crazy about Carlos since high school. Even when I was with the twins' father, he who shall not be named, I was thinking of Carlos.

I arrived at Chris's house just after ten in the morning. We'd agreed to meet then, because Carlos was at work and Chris skipped school to spend time with me. He hasn't seen me in almost a year, what's one day?

Chris waited for me on the steps. He looked behind me as I walked up the steps. "Where's your car?"

"I don't have a car. Thought we could take yours." I knew Chris had a learner's permit and Carlos bought him a car. Chris sent me pictures of the car, his school, and his computer club, so I'm involved in his life.

"I can't drive, except with an adult with a Massachusetts license." Chris shrugged. "I don't want to mess up my chances at driving before I take the test."

He had a point.

"I'll drive," I said.

I saw Chris hesitate. God only knows what Carlos told him about me.

"I'll go get the keys." That's what he said. "Where are we going?"

"I haven't had breakfast yet," I said. "Thought we could eat, then shop, then see what we want to do next."

"I just ate."

The kid had habits like Carlos. Get up, shower, eat; all before 9:00 a.m.

He got into the car. "I could drink coffee while you eat."

Nice offer, but I don't want him staring at me while I have breakfast.

"No," I said. "We'll shop first then eat lunch. We can buy you clothes, parts for your car, sports stuff. Where do you want to start?"

"Let's go to Midtown Mall. They got some shirts and stuff I like."

As soon as we enter the mall, two guys come up to Chris. He introduced them as Buzz and Bill, friends of his.

"Are you boys skipping school too?" I asked. "It seems like a good day for it."

"I left right after football season," said Buzz. "No use going to school if I can't play football."

"I used to date a football player." I put my hand on his arm. "He's the father of Chris's sisters."

"Yeah, most girls like football players." Buzz put his hand over mine.

"Ma, let's go," said Chris. "We need to get some coffee."

"You going to Dunkin Donut?" asked Bill. "We were just going there ourselves. Do you want to sit with us?"

"I'd love to get coffee with you guys," I said. "We can talk about school and you can tell me about Chris."

"We're going shopping," Chris said. "We'll take ours to go."

"C'mon." This from Bill. "I'd like to spend some time with your mom."

"No," said Chris. "We need to get shopping."

Chris's hands were fisted and his head shook. It's nice he wanted to spend time with me, without his friends. We all went into the store, Bill and Buzz got a table, and Chris and I got ours to go.

Chris said goodbye to his friends and we went to Target. We bought pants and shirts and shoes. I wanted to get Chris a new, better phone so we went to look at the selection.

"Now you don't have to sneak it around, I want you to have a decent phone with a data plan," I told him.

"I'm on Dad's plan," he said. "It's got data, but sometimes not enough."

"Do you want to go on a plan with me?" I had a pretty good one.

"No, I think I'll stay on Dad's plan," Chris said. "In case you have to go away again."

"I don't intend to go away again." I picked up the latest phone. "But let me buy you a good phone so that you can always contact me."

"You didn't intend to go away the first time." Chris moved away from me, still looking at the display case. "But you did."

"Sometimes things happen that we don't anticipate." I placed my arm around him. "I was sick, I needed to get better. Now I am."

"Are you going to move in with Dad and me?"

"We're talking about it. I'd also like to get Charity and Patrice to live with us."

"You said that when we talked on the phone. You said that's why you were coming back. You've been saying that for six months."

"I know," I said. "But it's complicated."

He continued to move away from me.

I followed him. "You know that you're my number one son, don't you?"

"I'm your only son." It was an old joke.

Chris continued to look at the items in the display case. He stopped and pointed. "I've been looking at that wristband. It tells you how many steps you take in a day, counts calories, and checks on your sleep. If I'm going to go out for sports, it'd be a big help."

I looked at the wristband and all its faces. My credit card was maxed out with the phone and the clothes. The wristband, secured to the display case by a thick strap, sat above other bands in the locked case. I looked around. The clerk who got us the phone had disappeared. I kneeled down; the lock, a simple one, could be opened with a credit card or any flat, inflexible item. The locks are made this way; they need to keep out the idle browser, but be easy enough for a fifteen-an-hour employee to open when needed.

Chris wandered over to look at videogames.

I joined him in front of the games; I didn't recognize most of them. "Do you play these games?" I asked him. I realized how little I knew about my own son.

"No. Mostly play online."

We left electronics and walked through the grocery aisles.

"Anything you want to eat?" I asked.

He picked up and put down a bunch of bananas. "Have you and Dad talked about your moving back home with us?"

"Not yet. I've only been home two days." We got in line for the checkout. "But we've always lived together before."

"Before you went away."

"Has your dad got a new girlfriend?" That would complicate matters.

"No, he's still married to you." Chris placed the items on the belt to go to the cashier. "But he doesn't talk about you much."

I don't know how to answer that.

We loaded the purchases into the car and I started it.

"Can we go to lunch now?" This from Chris.

"We were just at Dunkin Donuts an hour or so ago."

"That was just a snack," said Chris. "I'm still hungry. Can we go to the Chinese place?"

I drove across the parking lot and parked in front of the Chinese place.

I grabbed my purse from the back. "Well, if you're going to eat again, you may need this." I pulled the fancy wristband that Chris wanted from my purse and gave it to him.

"Where'd you get this?" Chris turned the box over. "And why is it in your purse?"

"At Target," I said. "I got it for you."

"I didn't see it at checkout. Did you pay for it?"

"Of course I paid for it." I took the box from him and opened it. "Try it on."

Chris put the wristband on. He's still staring at it when we go into the restaurant.

We took a booth in the back. The waitress came over and we both ordered lunch specials and tea.

"How is school going?" I asked.

"Okay. I skipped today to be with you."

"Is that going to be a problem?"

"No, I can keep up even if I'm not there." Chris shrugged. "I'd like to go out for track though, and I need to keep my grades up for that."

"And this will help." I tapped the fitness band, now on his wrist. "You can keep track of your exercise and your speed."

"I can't believe I got one. Dad said it was too expensive." Chris turned his wrist back and forth. I felt like the best mom in the world.

The waitress brought our food. We dug into the chicken fingers, rice, and sweet and sour soup. Chris told me a story about a kid at school. He had problems with his legs, had several operations, and still swings out his hip when he runs. When this kid, stuck with the awful name Cedric, went to try out for the track team, everyone laughed at him. Turned out he could jump hurdles better than most, though he's not fast or coordinated. And his funny gait made people think he wasn't going to make the jump but he did, every time. Chris is a good storyteller, something he got from me.

The waitress came to leave the bill. I asked for more tea. Chris looked at his fitness band and noticed it was down to eighteen percent; he'll have to charge it when he gets home. The waitress came back, no tea, and said that my credit card had been declined.

"Are you sure? I just used it in Target."

"Yes, ma'am. I tried it twice."

I took back that card and laid down my other credit card.

"Do you need money, Mom?"

"No, Chris, I'm treating you today. Don't worry about it."

The waitress returned, with the tea, and laid down the tray with the credit card on it. This time, there's a receipt for my signature. Good, that card worked. I picked up the paper and signed my name. Chris looked down at the credit card.

"Mom, this card's got Dad's name on it."

"I know." I gave the signed copy to the waitress and put the card in my purse.

"Does Dad know you're using his card?"

"He won't mind me buying lunch for you."

"That's not what I asked." Chris took the band off his wrist and laid it on the table in front of me. "I don't want this if it gets you in trouble. Dad said it's too expensive."

I picked it up. "This band won't show up on Dad's credit card. It's my gift to you."

"Okay, I guess." Chris's phone hummed and he pulled it out of his pocket. "I'm going to the bathroom." He left.

I poured myself another cup of tea, enabled the GPS tracking system on his band, and connected it to my phone.

CHAPTER TEN

FREYA

"WHERE'D THE DOG COME FROM?" THOSE WERE THE first words Gabe said when he came home. No "hello," no "how was your day?".

I placed the food and water on the floor. "It's Chris's dog," I said.

"I know that." Gabe sat down at the table and pulled off his boots. "What's he doing here?"

"Chris left Alaska with Carlos," I said. "Carlos had to go out, didn't know when he'd be back, so he brought him here. I didn't have Patrice, so I let him stay."

We both agreed it was difficult with young children and a large dog, but sometimes we did it anyway.

"Carlos was here?"

I left the dog and went to sit at the table with my husband. "Bad day?"

"Carlos is being unreasonable. Wants me to lean on people who are slow to pay. That's not my job."

I reached out and took his hand. "If the job bothers you, you can quit. We'll make out somehow."

"How? We've got to support ourselves and two kids, and pay the lawyer for the custody stuff. And Stella's still dead, and we don't know what will happen with that."

"All that's true," I said. "But running yourself ragged won't help. You're still on disability, so there's some income. And I hear the florist is hiring. He pays cash too."

"Can you see me putting little seeds in little pots for a few dollars an hour?"

"I'll do it then. I can put little seeds in little pots. But then you'll have to take care of the dog."

It wasn't much of a joke, but Gabe laughed anyway.

I sat down across from him. "What are we going to do about Jade?"

"Why do we have to do anything about her?"

We'd had this discussion before. We'd never agreed about Jade. "I know she's your brother's child, and I love her like my own, but Jade has problems. She disrupts our lives and the lives of her children."

"Jade is our daughter, all legal." Gabe looked around the kitchen. "You been reading the runes again?"

"I don't need to read runes to know Jade brings trouble, even if she's our daughter and doesn't mean to. It happens."

"Jade's had a hard life," said Gabe. "Her parents died when she was five, we adopted her; she never felt she belonged anywhere." Gabe reached out and took my hand. "But she looks like she's in a good place now; she's looking great, went to rehab, even got her teeth fixed."

"Fixing her teeth won't fix everything that's wrong with her." I love Jade, but she only cares for Jade. She doesn't even acknowledge that anyone else exists.

"She needs help." The dog came over and laid his head in Gabe's lap, as if sensing he was upset. "Maybe we ought to give her a chance."

I needed to sprinkle some reality over Gabe's fantasy. "Jade has been back for one day. We don't know where she's been, or even where she's staying. We don't even know if she's back with Carlos and Chris."

Gabe pushed Alaska's head aside and stood up. "And if I quit working for Carlos, he may take it out on Jade."

"He wouldn't do that."

"We don't know that," said Gabe. "I'm just so tired. Tired of being responsible for everyone, tired of not having enough money, and tired of this court thing."

A loud knock shook the front door. I went to the window and saw Charity's lawyer and her assistant on the front porch. I told Gabe to stay where he was, and answered the door. Attorney Allen called earlier, and I told her that Charity was at daycare this afternoon. I told her again and gave her directions. She left.

"And I'm tired of all these people coming to the house and sticking their nose in our business." Gabe opened the front door and went out on the porch.

I decided that now was not a good time to tell him that I'd arranged to visit the Citizen Advocacy man this afternoon.

CHAPTER ELEVEN

GABE

I WAS SITTING ON THE PORCH, DRINKING COFFEE. IT'S cold in March, but the house seemed too small. Sometimes I just need to be alone.

Freya came to the door. "You can't sit out there all day. We have to meet with Richard from Citizen Advocacy."

"What's Citizen Advocacy?" I asked. Then I remembered the card that Bonnie left. "You mean the guy that changed his name? Are we supposed to meet him?"

"Yeah," said Freya. "I told you I was going to set up an appointment. He wants to meet us at the diner on the corner."

I didn't feel like moving. "Why can't he come here?"

Freya came out onto the porch with her coat and gloves on. "Because he's in a motorized scooter. He's handicapped, can't walk. We need to go to the diner to meet him. It's got a ramp."

I still didn't want to go, but I didn't want to argue with Freya more. It took us less than ten minutes to walk to the diner. When we arrived, the warm air smelled like fried onions and coffee. Richard was at a table on the east side, nearest the handicap ramp. I looked around. Guess the building was accessible, but no way he could have maneuvered the scooter between the tables, packed so close together.

Richard needed to move his scooter aside for us to sit down. The waitress came with coffee and had to do a left-hand pour. Richard ordered an English muffin and Freya and I stuck with coffee.

"Why'd you want to meet with us?" I asked.

"Court is this week," said Richard. "I wanted to talk to you before then. We can't get an advocate for you so soon, but I can come to court and support you."

"Are you okay?" I asked. He didn't look good.

"Just having a bad day." He smiled. "Some days are better than others."

He took a drink of his coffee. "As I said, I'm from Citizen Advocacy. We're a local volunteer organization that helps our people in the community. Bonnie Bates suggested I come see you."

"She left your card." I put my cup on the table. "We already got a lawyer and a social worker and Bonnie. Why do we need another person?"

"Bonnie's worried about Charity." He leaned forward as if telling me a secret. "She read about her father, George Banks, and his bringing a gun into the courthouse. She thought you might need some help right now."

I'd heard this routine before. People come into the house, offering support, and then they want to change things we do and "monitor" the kids and generally screw up our daily routine. Though Ms. Bonnie had been really nice to us and she worked hard to get Charity speaking so everyone could understand her.

"I still don't understand," said Freya.

"Citizen Advocacy provides advocates for adults and children. Given the present court case with Charity, Bonnie thought that you might use an advocate."

"And that'd be you?"

"No, I'm just the coordinator." He put a business card on the table. "My job is to match you with an advocate. Somebody who knows the court system."

"That might be good," I said. "I sometimes come out of court more confused than when I went in." I looked at his card, but didn't pick it up.

"If we match you with an advocate, that person will work for you and the kids. Provide rides, support, anything else you need. We're a matching service for friends. I have a person, a teacher, in mind to work with you," Richard said. "She knows about child development, and she can go to court with you and let folks know that you are doing things for the girls."

Marcy had talked about hiring an expert in child development to testify about how we parent. We didn't have the money to hire anyone, but maybe we could get this for free. I looked at Freya, who nodded her head.

"Okay, we'll give it a try." I picked up his card.

"You're going to court soon, right?" Richard said. "I'll be there, just to observe, so I can talk to the advocate about what needs to be done. We'll set up a time for you to meet her next week, if she agrees."

We shook hands.

"Do you need some help getting out of here?" asked Freya.

"No, I'm a pro at this," he said. "I just want to finish my muffin first."

We walked back to the house. As we arrived, Chris's car pulled in. I watched Chris get out of the passenger side and his mother, Jade, get out the driver's side. Last thing I knew, Jade didn't have a driving license. Carlos got out of the back.

"Pops, look what Ma got me." Chris showed me a band, about an inch thick, on his arm. "It's a wristband that tells me how many steps I've taken, gets emails and texts." He pressed the button on the side and words appeared on the tiny screen. Too small for me to read, but he seemed impressed.

"I've seen those on television," I said. "Everybody running around, trying to get their steps in for the day."

Jade stood in the yard. We stared at each other for a few moments.

"I brought Chris to pick up his dog," she said.

I unlocked and opened the door and Alaska came rushing out, as if he knew it was time to go home.

"Can we talk, Dad?" asked Jade. "About the girls."

Chris put the leash on Alaska and took him to his car. Carlos got into the driver's seat and they left.

"Will you give me a ride home?" Now Jade expected me to drive her around. "Please. We can talk on the ride."

"Let me talk to your mother." I signaled Freya and we went into the back room. I told her I was going to give Jade a ride home and talk about the girls. She pointed out that Jade had just arrived, with a ride. I agreed, but wanted to talk to Jade.

"Do you want to come with us?" I asked.

"I have to go next door and pick up Patrice," she said. "You go without me and we can talk about it later."

I grabbed the keys to the Ford pickup and went outside to Jade. She hadn't moved.

I walked by her. "Let's go" was all I said.

She followed me to the garage and I opened the door. "We're taking the pickup," I said. "Just got it registered."

"Still fixing up old trucks, I see." Jade stopped talking.

We were both thinking about Stella, dead in a vehicle I worked on.

"I'm sorry, Dad." Jade got in the truck.

"Nothing to be sorry about." I backed into the street. "Nothing I did caused Stella's death. The truck ran fine."

We drove a couple of blocks in silence. We're not going to get anything resolved if we don't talk.

I pulled up to the stop sign and looked at Jade. "What did you want to say?"

"Dad, I think you and Ma have done a great job raising Charity and taking care of Patrice." Jade fiddled with her seatbelt. "But there's a reason Stella adopted Charity, instead of you. You've raised enough kids; it's time for you to retire."

She's trying to convince me that her taking the kids was for my own good. I'm old, but I'm not stupid. I didn't say anything.

"I'm sober and I'm looking for work," she continued. "I could take care of the kids. Carlos would help me."

Even if Jade had taken care of her drug problem, she still had parenting problems. Her problems with the twins started before she got involved with drugs. She must think my memory's bad too.

"Your mom and I can raise the kids," I said. "We've done it until now and we'll continue doing it. Have you asked Carlos about raising the kids with you?"

"We've talked about it." Jade twirled her hair around her fingers.

That's her tell. She's lying, or at least not telling the whole truth.

"Has Carlos said he'll help you?"

"We're still talking about it," she said. "He's a little upset that I've been talking to Chris without him knowing."

"Did he know you took Chris shopping today?" My guess is he didn't.

"What does it matter what Carlos knows or doesn't know? He's not the boss of me and we're talking about my grandchildren." Jade picked at the seatbelt.

I started to slow down for another stop sign.

"If you're going to raise children with him, you've got to talk to him," I said. "You can't just make decisions that are convenient for you."

"I am thinking about it. And I don't want to talk with you about it anymore." She unbuckled her seatbelt and opened the door.

"Jade, stop." I reached for her, to pull her back into the truck. The door shut behind her.

"Get your hands off me. You can't tell me what to do."

I slowed down. "Jade, what's the matter? Can we just talk? We both want what's best for the kids."

"Sometimes it's so hard." Jade stared out the windshield. "You and Mom think I'm a screwup."

"We don't think that." Though I think I'd said something similar, just that morning. But I did love Jade and wanted things to work out for her.

"You don't even say that like you mean it," she said. "I'm just a problem for you. You never gave me a chance to parent or get to know my kids."

She slid away from me, toward the door. I was slowing down but the truck was still moving. She hadn't buckled her seatbelt again.

"We'll decide this in court." As she said it, she opened the door again, slid off the seat and onto the road. I heard her scream.

I pulled the truck in front of her and got out. The car behind us, a white Nissan, pulled over also. Jade lay on her side, in the dirt by the side of the road. I noticed blood on her pants and her hands and sand in her hair.

"Jade, are you all right?" I knelt down beside her. Brown shoes came into view. The man from the white Nissan was standing over us.

"Leave me alone. Leave me alone." Jade pushed me away from her. "I don't want anything to do with you."

"I've called 911. The police are on their way." This from the brown shoes.

The police must have been close, because they arrived less than five minutes later. By then, Jade was standing up, crying softly. The police officer separated us and spoke to Jade. I could see her gesturing and crying. The police officer gave her tissues.

The police officer came over to me. "She says that you are her father."

"Yes, sir." I just wanted this to be over.

"What happened?" This police officer had a pen and paper for his notes.

"She fell out of the truck."

He flipped back over some pages in the notes. "She says that you were having an argument."

"Yes, sir."

"And she fell out of the truck."

I didn't say anything.

"She refused an ambulance." He closed the notepad and put it in his pocket. "Says she doesn't want to ride with you. I'll take her home."

Jade got into the cruiser and left.

CHAPTER TWELVE

GABE

I DON'T KNOW WHAT JADE'S GOING TO DO OR WHAT SHE was thinking, leaving in the cruiser. I can't think about that now, I have another appointment.

I hurried downtown, to a one-room office over a secondhand store. Sounds like it could be the line in a song, but that's where Stan Sykes kept an office. He'd been a cop for twenty years, retired, got bored, and then started a one-man private eye shop.

I was the only person on the second floor, with three doors; one marked "private," one marked "Mark Blast, CPA," and one marked "Stan Sykes, Private Investigations." I'd hire a PI that worked out of a tiny office, but wondered who would hire a CPA that looked so poor. Never had any money, so that wasn't a problem I was going to have soon.

I knocked on Stan's door and a voice that drank too many whiskies and smoked too many cigarettes told me to come in. The room was large, with two arched windows overlooking Main Street. Real wood floors showed that someone had once spent some money on the place. But not on the furnishings. A battered metal desk, some file cabinets, and two wooden chairs looked like they had been bought secondhand. A brand-new laptop sat on the desk. Stan stood up when I entered and the chair he used looked like the most expensive thing in the room. Even more than the laptop. It looked like leather and it was thickly padded and had rows of buttons making a pattern up the back. I must have been staring at the chair.

"When I left the police department, I decided that I would never again sit in an uncomfortable chair." That was Stan's greeting. "I've got a recliner at home and this ergonomic chair here. Sit down."

I realized this last statement was directed at me and took a seat in one of the wooden chairs. My knees rose high and I shifted to the right and almost slid off the front of the chair.

Stan laughed. "My personal joke. The front legs are an inch shorter than the back legs. Makes people get to the point, so they can get out of the chair."

I stood up and he came around the desk and shook my hand. "I'm not going to torture you with my furniture," he said. "Let's go downstairs, eat at the Blind Pig. My treat."

"I thought I was supposed to pay you," I said.

"You get the family rate, because you're Mike's brother," he said.

We needed to get this settled now. "I don't have any money. I can't pay you, even at a discount rate."

"I know," said Stan. "And I don't have time to take on another case anyway. We'll talk, make a plan, and you can get information. I can run background checks and help you make plans. But that's it. I don't want to get between you and Jade."

Stan was, first and foremost, a friend of my brother, now dead for almost forty years. My brother was Jade's biological father and Stan had always looked out for her. I didn't want to interfere with that.

He headed for the door. I followed.

"What if Jade asks for your help?" I asked.

"I'll tell her the same thing. I'll talk to her and run background checks. But, as neither of you hired me, nothing is confidential. That okay with you?"

I nodded. I wanted Jade to get what she needed too.

We walked to the Blind Pig and the bartender waved us to the back. We sat in a booth, separated from the rest of the place by a divider.

"Glen saves this booth for me. I do most of my business here. Except for the people I make sit in my chairs."

A young man appeared, wearing an apron tied over his jeans. "What will you be having to drink?" he asked. He handed us both menus.

"You go first," I said to Stan.

"He knows what I want. Gin and tonic. And the burger special of the day."

I hadn't gone out to eat in quite a while. Seemed like a waste of money to me, and Freya liked cooking for the family. Couldn't remember the last time I had alcohol.

"I'll have a beer," I said.

"What kind of beer?" asked the waiter. "We have all the commercial beers, some local breweries, specialty beers."

He said some things after that but I lost track. Back in high school, we just drank what was cheapest. Since then, I just drank what I could get. I must have looked confused, because he stopped talking.

"He'll have the steel head beer." This from Stan.

We studied the menus until the young man returned with the drinks. Which was all of three minutes. Either the service was great, or Stan was a good tipper. I ordered the burger of the day too. It just seemed easier.

"How is Jade doing?" That was Stan's first question.

"She just got back to town," I said. "I've only seen her a few times. Says she's clean and sober and she looks good."

"Glad to hear it. I worry about her; she's had a hard life. Sometimes I think things may have turned out different."

"How?" I asked.

"Don't know exactly," said Stan. "If you hadn't adopted her, maybe the misses and I would have. Strange to think about a daughter." Stan was the father of three sons.

"Jade and I got into an argument today." I told him about Jade and the truck.

"Yeah, that little girl started out tough. Still don't understand why her parents left her alone that night. Even if they only expected to be gone a little while, why didn't they take her with them?" He shook his head. "Doesn't seem like she can get a break."

I wish people would stop asking that question. I decided to change the topic.

"But that's not why I'm here." I played with my glass, twirling it between my fingers. Realized I'd not yet taken a drink, though Stan's glass was half empty. I took a sip. Not bad. "I'm here about Jade's daughter, Stella."

"Yeah, I heard about her." Now Stan was stirring his drink that didn't need stirring. "Sorry about her death. Hope I can help."

"Thanks. I don't know any other private eyes and thought you might help because of my brother, Mike." I stopped talking. "I know Mike's been dead for most of Jade's life, but I do appreciate you coming around, checking on Jade all these years."

"I help out when I can," said Stan. "And, of course, I'll help now. Just so long as you know I'll help Jade too. Might even share information. If that's okay with you, we can plan how to proceed."

"Okay. Though, depending on what happens, I may stop talking to you at some point."

"No problem. But I'll need to work you around my paying clients."

From the looks of his office, he had a lot of free time. Maybe I was being unfair. Or maybe he lived off his police pension and did this to fill his days. His wife died three months after he retired. And he hadn't mentioned any of his sons.

"Stella died in a car accident." I stopped. It was hard to talk about.

"Had she been drinking?" Stan asked the logical question.

"Nope. She was coming from work. First thing they did was check her blood alcohol level, even though it was the middle of the afternoon. They took her blood at the hospital."

"So she survived the accident?"

"Yeah, but she never came to after she got to the hospital. Died the next day." I could feel tears running down my cheeks. I was getting better. Two weeks ago, there would have been snot and wailing.

Stan handed me a napkin. I wiped my face. He waited.

"At first, the police thought it was her fault," I continued. "Then they found a nick in the brake line."

"A nick?"

"A hole. Thought at first it hit something when she went off the road."

"What changed their mind?" Stan was a good guy. He just assumed the police had changed their mind.

"I told them there was nothing wrong with the brake line. I fixed that car myself. I've always taken care of that car; it's the only car I ever bought new. Of course, all my kids and grandkids could check the oil and use a tire gauge by the time they went to school."

"Even the girls."

"Especially the girls. Don't want the car breaking down and some loser trying to fix it. Take advantage of the situation." I'd had nightmares both ways. Mechanics ripping the girls off for huge sums of money and perverts taking advantage of them being alone in a dark place. Not that all my worrying had helped Stella.

"You're sure the line wasn't damaged that last time you fixed the car?" asked Stan.

I nodded. "And Chris and I did work on the car just before she took it out." I realized I was twirling my glass again and put my hands under the table. "Chris was there with me. Even if my eyes are getting old, he would have seen a cut line."

"And it was a new car? In good condition?"

I smiled. "It was a 1994 El Camino. Only new car I ever bought. I've worked on it all these years." I took a sip of my beer. "Can't work on the new cars, too many computers. But the El Camino was in great shape."

We both stopped talking when the waiter slid our burgers in front of us.

"What about your job with Carlos? Piss anybody off lately?" Stan was staring at me. He used to be a cop, so he knew about Carlos and his bookmaking operation.

"I just make deliveries and collect money for Carlos. I don't piss people off." Not exactly true, but close enough.

"But you do collect when they lose," said Stan. "Anybody get angry at having to pay you?"

"Most people don't pay any attention to me. I'm just the hands that collect the money and deliver the packages. And then they'd have to connect me to Stella." I stopped talking for a minute, thinking about how easy that would be to do. "Stella's name was Leary, but there's a crapload of us in town. My grandpa was one of fourteen children."

"Still, it's something I'll look into," Stan said. "Who else would hurt Stella? She have any enemies? Old boyfriends?"

"Stella had custody of Celeste's kid, Charity. She worked and took care of the kids. Not much extra time."

"Gabe, that's bullshit."

I looked at Stan. He was staring at me.

"Stella was twenty-four years old," Stan said. "She had to have friends and, if she got any of Jade's good looks, the guys would notice her."

"She worked at the diner from 6:00 a.m. to 2:00 p.m. Tuesday through Saturday. She sometimes waitressed here, on the weekends. She took care of Charity. She was a good kid."

"She was a young woman. She had friends, and maybe lovers, that you don't know about." Stan took a bite of his burger. "This is good." He put it down. "She didn't spend all her time at home or at work." This wasn't a question.

"She had a couple of girlfriends, Tina Watson and Danielle Potts. They went out together every Thursday night, so we took care of

Charity. We had a block party last year and Stella came with Adam Watson, Tina's brother."

"That'll give you a place to start. You need to talk to the girls. And to this Watson kid."

My phone vibrated. I checked and saw Carlos wanted me to do another pickup tonight. I'd deal with that after I finished with Stan.

"You might also want to talk to the people that Stella worked with." Stan took another bite of his burger. "If you're going to dig into Stella's life, you may find some things you don't know and won't like. Are you ready for that?"

"Yeah, I am." I picked up a French fry and pointed it at him. "But you better be sure I get the information right."

Stan and I finished our meal and left the restaurant. Stan walked me to my truck. I checked the text from Carlos. Somehow, Antonio had come up with the money he owed and Carlos wanted me to pick it up tonight, before Antonio lost it on some other bet.

I drove out to the country club. I'm not usually there at night, when the parking lot is full. The valet wasn't the one I usually deal with, but he'd been filled in, because he let me park in back, near the dumpster. He didn't want me going through the dining room when it was full, so I entered the kitchen from the alley.

Lots more noise and action than during the day. Steam rose from multiple prep stations and from the dishwashers, coating everything in a fine mist. Waiters ran back and forth, picking up food and prepping salads. Gas fires raised the temperature in the kitchen, despite the open door letting in the cold March air.

I looked around for Antonio and jumped out of the way when a white-coated person yelled at me; he had a hot pan in his hand, so I didn't argue. I tried to ask him where Antonio was, but the noise level made talking difficult.

"Come with me." Somebody yelled this in my ear, grabbed my arm, and dragged me into the storeroom that served as Antonio's office. It was cooler in here, but I had to wipe the sweat off my face. Antonio stood in front of me, a plaster cast on his left hand.

He went to his desk, unlocked the drawer, and threw a bundle of cash on the top. "Here's the full five thousand," he said. "I don't want to see you again."

I picked up the cash. "What happened to your hand?"

"Broken fingers," he said. "As if you didn't know."

I didn't know, but he obviously thought I did.

Antonio continued talking. "My boss was not happy when your friends showed up this afternoon." He rubbed the two fingers not in a cast. "They broke my left hand, so I could still work and pay off my debt."

"My friends?" I asked.

"Yeah," said Antonio. "I can't think of anyone else I pissed off lately. Except Carlos."

FRIDAY

MARCH 13, 2020

CHAPTER THIRTEEN

GABE

Freya put the letter on the table in front of me. "Don't forget, we have to be in court today."

Today was a hearing about temporary custody. After Stella died, there was enough money left from her life insurance for us to get a lawyer and file for custody. Knew Banks was trying to get out of jail and I wasn't going to let him get his hands on Charity. They'd probably be living in his car and dealing drugs.

Marcy had filed for custody of Patrice and this was the first hearing on that matter. I thought I'd cut down on going to the courthouse if we did both kids at the same time. Now Charity's dad wanted them heard separately, though his girlfriend, former attorney Tracy Christenson, kept threatening to file papers on Patrice.

All this went through my head when Freya put the letter in front of me. "I know," was what I said. "I guess I need to go get dressed for court."

Freya's already dressed for court, with her blue dress and her pearls. I went up to our bedroom and she'd laid out my clothes on the bed. My good shoes pinched my feet, because sometimes my feet swell up at night. Nobody over sixty should ever be required to wear a tie. Though I've done it enough times that I can tie a decent knot without help.

Freya came up to the bedroom to help me into the gray blazer. I looked in the mirror, at the two of us. We look like two old people who shouldn't be raising more kids at our age. I pulled back my shoulders and Freya straightened up. We're going to try to convince the judge that we are just the people to raise Charity and Patrice.

We took the bus to the courthouse. It costs twenty bucks to park near the Worcester courthouse because all of the handicap places are filled all the time. One time, I even saw a police cruiser parked in the handicapped place. That's how bad the parking is. We got off the bus and walked the last block to the courthouse. My feet, already pinched by my shoes, hurt like hell. I was glad when we got inside and were early enough that there were places for both of us on the benches. I saved Freya's place while she went into the registrar's office to let them know we were here.

I heard a buzzing and Richard Fontaine, the guy from Citizen Advocacy, went by on his scooter. He went to the end of the hallway, turned around, and came back to me. He stopped in front of me. A large backpack hung off the back of his scooter.

"How are you doing today?" he asked.

"Nervous. Court makes me nervous." I looked around for Freya.

"Maybe I can help," he said. "Or at least sit with you and be on your side."

"Listen, Mr. Paoletti." I didn't know what to say next.

"It's Fontaine, Richard Fontaine. I recently changed my name. Please call me Richard."

I'd never heard of an adult man changing his name. He seemed a little embarrassed about it and smiled. His smile was crooked. Where the hell was Freya?

"But I interrupted you," said Richard. "What were you going to ask me?"

I couldn't remember, so I asked, "Why'd you go down to the end of the corridor and turn around?"

"This courthouse isn't made for scooters," he said.

"Morning, Richard," said Freya, joining us. "Well, we're on the docket today."

That's happened before too. We got all dressed up, rode the bus, and the court didn't know we were coming. Nobody pulled a file, so we got sent home.

"Thought you might like some support. Even if I don't say anything, it's nice to know that someone is on your side." Richard leaned down to adjust something on the scooter.

Freya pulled a paper from her purse. "We're in Courtroom Seven." She waved toward the end of the corridor. "I think it's down there."

Richard had to turn the scooter around again, which was confusing because the corridors were full up with people. Now everyone was watching us go into the courtroom. And I don't like to be watched.

Richard tried to fit his scooter in the back of the courtroom, between the wooden seats and the door. Part of it jutted out into the aisle. We sat in the last row, just in front of him. The court officer came over to talk to Richard and took his backpack off the hanger. He took everything out of the pack and put it on the table in the back of the room. Pens, paper, a reusable coffee cup, and some tubing I didn't want to know about. He put it all back in the pack but kept the pack on the table.

"Sir, you need to get out of the aisle," said the guard.

"Where do you want me to go?" asked Richard.

The guard had him take the scooter into the middle of the courtroom, turn around, and back in. By then, half a dozen people were by the door, waiting to get in. Part of the scooter was still in the aisle. The court officer threw up his hands and left.

Court is mostly waiting for things to happen. When I see them on TV, rushing in and out of courtrooms, making objections, and arguing with the judge, I just laugh. Before I came the first time, I expected the judge to listen to everybody and ask lots of questions. It's not like that at all. Everybody goes into the courtroom at the same time and you sit and listen to people whine and argue and ask the judge for dumb things until your case is called. Some judges read everything you wrote about the case before they heard you. The lawyer we hired for the girls had us write down everything that happened with Stella and Celeste and she put it in the court papers. The first judge we had read everything and gave us custody.

Today's judge asked lots of questions, like maybe he didn't read anything. I guess judges are busy, but you think he'd know something about his cases. The first two cases went quickly. They were uncontested divorces and both the husband and wife or, in the other case, both wives, had lawyers. The lawyers told the judge what the agreement said, he approved it, and they were divorced.

The third case was more interesting. Neither the husband nor the wife had lawyers and they'd done their own agreement. The husband made a hundred fifty thousand dollars a year as an engineer and the wife made thirty thousand as a secretary. They had four kids and had been married twenty years. The wife got to keep the house and she would get five hundred a week until the youngest child was twenty-one, about seven years from now. This didn't sound fair to me, she got to raise the kids and he kept most of the money. Guess it didn't sound good to the judge either; he kept talking about "equitable division" which sounds like, and I guess means, equal. The husband kept saying that both parties had agreed to the arrangements, but the judge wasn't buying it. They didn't get divorced that day.

Most of the rest of the cases, the judge heard from people and pretty much kept things the way they were and continued them to another day. I hoped he would do that with us, too, so we could keep Charity and Patrice. We were in the courtroom, with only about ten people still there, when Celeste and Jade entered the room. Jade looked better than when she was at the house. Her hair was pulled back with a silver clip and she wore a deep red suit with a short skirt. It was Celeste I had to look twice at. She had on a long-sleeved blouse and a denim shirt. She'd had her hair curled and it had some kind of sheen to it. She was wearing makeup that didn't make her look so pale. This was the best I'd seen her in years. They both sat in the back of the room, across the aisle from us.

The room was clearing out. Because our case involved custody of a minor, we went last. I knew we were getting close when Marcy walked into the courtroom and took her seat. My hands were sweating. I didn't know what was going to happen. This judge seemed to just continue things, without making an actual decision.

The lady sitting next to the judge called, "The Case of Charity Leary."

They brought Banks out from the back of the room, in handcuffs. The judge asked us to identify ourselves. Banks said he was the father; Celeste, the mother. I identified myself as the great-grandfather and guardian. Then Jade said she was the grandmother and that caused some confusion. The judge kept asking questions so we couldn't explain that Freya and I were married and Jade was our daughter. Finally, the judge stopped asking questions and let Marcy explain.

"My clients are the great-grandparents and they have custody of Charity because their granddaughter, Stella, was her adoptive mother. Stella and Charity lived with them. After Stella's death, my clients filed for and got custody of Charity. A few weeks ago, the biological mother of Charity and Patrice, that's Celeste Leary, dropped Patrice off at my clients' home and they have filed for custody of her also. Celeste Leary is the biological mother of both children and Jade Vega is their grandmother."

The judge looked at us over his glasses. "If the child was adopted, why are the biological parents here?"

"I want my daughter back," said Celeste. "My mother will help me." She gestured toward Jade.

"And you, sir?" The judge turned toward George Banks.

"I'm the father," said Banks. "The other judge said I could have a trial about Charity."

"The other judge?" This judge looked at Montoya, Banks's attorney. I knew that judges liked to talk to lawyers, not real people.

"Mr. Banks recently filed a motion to reopen the termination of parental rights." Montoya laid a paper on the table. "This is the allowed order for a new trial in juvenile court."

That was all the judge needed to hear. He leaned back and stared at all of us. "I'm sending this back to juvenile court," he said. "I won't take any action until their case is finished."

Montoya started to pick up his papers. I guess he'd accomplished what he needed to do.

"When do we come back here?" Jade asked.

"After the juvenile court matter is settled," said the judge. "I can't do anything while it's pending." He turned to Montoya again. "When's the next date in juvenile court?"

"Next Tuesday, in Meredith," said Montoya.

"Case adjourned until next Tuesday in Meredith Juvenile Court." The judge didn't bang his gavel, but the case was over. "The court officer will give you a reminder of when and where to appear."

"Your Honor," said Marcy. "There is no juvenile court order on Patrice. My clients, Jesus and Freya Leary, have temporary guardianship. That needs to be extended."

"So ordered." The judge gathered his robe and left by a door at the back of the courtroom.

I followed Montoya out of the courtroom. "Attorney Montoya," I said.

He kept walking, like he had more important things to do. I can walk fast, as long as I don't have to walk too far. I caught up with him and put my hand on his sleeve. He stopped.

"Please don't touch me." He moved his arm back and shook it, like I got dirt on it or something.

Jade walked past us, muttering to herself.

"Attorney Montoya," I said. "I want to talk about the girls. About what will happen to them."

"Your attorney and I will discuss that." He picked a speck of dust off his sleeve. "Perhaps next week, in juvenile court."

Marcy and Freya came up to me.

"Let's go," said Marcy. "You got what you want, you got custody. We'll work out the rest of the details later."

She was right; we still had both girls with us. Sometimes, just staying even is the best you can do. We turned to go.

Jade stood in front of me, with Celeste a few steps behind her.

"You didn't let me say anything." Jade's voice rose at the end of the sentence. "I'm trying to be a good mother, to take care of my kids, and you won't let me."

"Mom, let's go." Celeste put her hand on Jade's shoulder.

"No, I have something to say." Jade shook off the hand and stepped closer to me. "I'm younger than you, I'm smarter than you, and I know things you don't want me to say. And I fight dirty."

The court officer came out of Courtroom Seven, maybe because Jade's voice carried down the corridor.

"Ma'am, you can't be making so much noise outside the court-room," the officer said.

In an instant, Jade's face grew softer and her shoulders relaxed. "Oh, officer, I'm so glad you're here," she said. "This man won't let me get out of the courthouse. He's insisting that I talk to him and I don't want to."

"Sir, please stand back," said the officer.

"What's going on?" Marcy came up and stood directly behind me.

"Ma'am, please get out of the way." The court officer stood between Jade and me.

"I'm this man's attorney, what's going on?"

"Your client tried to accost me in the hallway." Jade's voice was not as loud, but it was filled with venom.

"If you are feeling unsafe, I can walk you to your car." The officer put back his shoulder and hitched up his belt as he addressed Jade.

"That would be most kind," said Jade. "I am a little frightened. What's your name?"

"Jorge," said the officer. "Do you need anything before we leave?"

"No, I've got my things. Let's go."

Marcy put her hand on my shoulder. "Let them go. We don't need a confrontation in the courthouse."

I wanted to say something, but was afraid it would be the wrong thing.

Jorge and Jade continued their conversation as they left the courthouse. Guess Jade's fear of me didn't extend to her daughter, as she left Celeste standing in the middle of the hallway. She took the bus home with us.

CHAPTER FOURTEEN

JADE

THE COURT OFFICER WAS SO NICE TO ME; HE HELPED ME out of the courthouse and into my car. My dad had no right to hassle me in the courthouse. He's always trying to tell me how to live my life. I started the car and waved at the court officer before he went back inside. Of course, I'm not really leaving. I'm in Carlos's car and needed to wait for him. I took out my phone to see if I had any messages while I was in court.

The passenger door opened and Tracy Christensen slid into the car. This woman had some nerve, hooking up with Charity's father, threatening my mother, and now getting into my car.

"What the hell do you want?" I saw no reason to be polite to her.

"I need to talk to you," she said. "Hope you're more reasonable than your mother."

"My husband's coming out of the courthouse any minute. I don't have time to talk to you." I looked down at my phone again, as if I had important information there.

Tracy took the phone from me and put it on the dashboard of the car.

"That's assault." I know lots about the legal system, more than some lawyers. "I could have you arrested."

"But you won't," she said. "You want to hear what I have to say."

I had my doubts about that, but what's she going to do in the courthouse parking lot?

I looked down at her leg. "I thought you were on a monitoring anklet."

"I am." She pulled up her pant leg to show me the black device, with lights blinking on the side. "But here is one place I'm authorized to go. I can stretch my time out. They usually don't check on me unless I'm very late."

She's talking like we're best buds. We're not friends. She's trying to take my grandchildren away from the family. I took my phone off the dashboard.

"I think we can work together," said Tracy. "About Charity and Patrice."

As if I would talk to her for any other reason. I'm smarter and more experienced than my mother. I'm not going to be intimidated, even if she went to law school.

"We can work out something," Tracy continued. "You and George could be co-guardians of both girls."

"Both girls? Patrice isn't Banks's child."

"But wouldn't it be easier to just deal with one father? Then the girls could always stay together, with you or with me and Banks."

"What's in this for you?" She had to have an angle.

"I love George. If I'm with George, that includes his children. I need to develop a relationship with them."

"But you don't know them. You're only doing this because of George. At least I've been around, until recently, and know about the family."

The family. That's the issue here. My father always told me that family is everything. We can fight among ourselves and want different things, but when an outsider tries to butt in, we need to stick together. George Banks was an outsider, because he led Celeste on and then left her for another woman. Who then left him, so there is some justice in the world. And Tracy, she didn't even know the family. I was done talking.

"Get out of my car. You're not part of the family and I don't have to talk to you." I leaned across Tracy and opened the passenger door.

Her monitor beeped. I don't know if it meant her time was up, or it just beeped once in a while, but she looked down at it. She got out of the car.

"We haven't finished talking." She slammed the car door.

Just in time. Carlos came to the driver's door and opened it.

"Get in the passenger seat," he said. "I'm driving."

It's probably a good idea, so I get in the other side and he gets in behind the wheel.

"What was that about?" He turned to look at me.

"Nothing,"

"That was Tracy Christensen, Banks's girlfriend."

As if I don't know that. "She wanted to talk to me about the girls."

"What about the girls?"

"She wanted to make a deal, where Banks and I share custody."

"Share custody?" Carlos was persistent.

"Yeah, like co-guardians. The girls could spend time with me and Banks." I slipped my phone into my purse. "I said no."

"Are you sure you said no? Is that what she understood?"

"Contrary to what you believe, I can be clear when I say no. She's not family and we need to stick together as a family."

"Don't forget that. It's the most important thing." Carlos put the car in drive and we went out of the parking lot.

Rather than turning toward the cobbler shop, we got on the highway.

"Where are we going?" I asked.

"To the mall," he said. "If you're going to ask for visits, you need to look like you're ready for them. That means we need to buy some stuff for the kids."

"I could buy a red dress for Charity and a blue dress for Patrice, both the same pattern. Maybe buy them both pajamas with feet in them and ducks or teddy bears on the front."

"They've got clothes," said Carlos. "I was thinking about beds and a highchair."

We could use those too.

CHAPTER FIFTEEN

JADE

AFTER WE FINISHED SHOPPING, I WENT TO CARLOS'S house with him. We're getting closer to moving in together. Carlos was getting used to the idea, I sensed his moods. Chris was at school, so it was just Carlos and me.

Carlos lives above the cobbler shop. It's a big apartment, two floors. Plenty of room for Charity and Patrice to have a room of their own. It's laid out a bit strange; a central corridor on both floors with rooms off to the side. On the second floor, the kitchen and dining room on one side, with the living room and Carlos's bedroom on the other side. The third floor had only three rooms because of the pitched roof.

Carlos put together a late lunch and I checked my email. Carlos kept looking over my shoulder. Not that I have anything incriminating in my emails.

Carlos put a tuna sandwich on whole wheat toast in front of me. "How did it go in court today?" he asked.

"Nothing changed." I picked up the sandwich. "You got chips?"

To my surprise, he did. Vinegar, my favorite.

"Vinegar is Chris's favorite," he said. "Did you talk to Freya and Gabe?"

"Not really," I said. "They weren't much into talking." I took a bite of the sandwich. Not bad. "They had some new guy with them, he's handicapped."

"A new lawyer?"

"I don't think so. He said he's from some place called Citizen Advocacy. He said he recently changed his name."

"Why'd he change his name?" Carlos took the lid off the organic, fat-free yogurt. "That's unusual for a guy."

"I thought so too. Bet I know how to find out." I pulled the computer closer to me.

"Don't get tuna on my computer," said Carlos.

"I won't." I can do more than one thing at a time.

I pulled out a business card from my purse and typed in "Richard Fontaine." Bunch of stuff about a kid that disappeared twenty years ago. "Not much here."

"Which name you look under?" asked Carlos.

"The name on the card," I said. Duh.

"Why don't you look under his other name?"

I'm ahead of him. I spelled it wrong, so it took me a few tries. Then it came up under "Richard Paoletti." I knew I had the right one because his pictures were there, on that scooter he rode.

"Here he is," I said. "His father was a lawyer, killed somebody at the courthouse." I kept going. "Dozens and dozens of stories about him."

"I remember reading about that," said Carlos.

As if he read regularly. Probably saw it on one of those streaming gossip shows.

Carlos kept talking. "He shot his pregnant girlfriend or something. There was some girl-on-girl action there, too."

Yup, he definitely got his information from social media.

I scanned through the entries for a few minutes. "It says here he killed the surrogate carrying his child. He changed his mind."

"Wasn't the surrogate married to another woman?" Leave it to Carlos to get stuck on that fact.

"Yeh, it says Richard gave some evidence that led to his arrest." I scrolled down some more. "His lawyer father hasn't gone to trial yet, so there's lots of 'alleged' and 'suspicions' language. No wonder the guy changed his name."

Carlos started picking up the rest of the food from the table.

"Wait a minute, I haven't finished." I took the yogurt and the spoon out of his hand.

Carlos placed his stuff in the sink. "Why didn't he change his name to Smith or Johnson if he wanted to hide who he was?"

"Looks like he was born Richard Fontaine. There're articles about a boy by that name missing for twenty years. Something fishy about his adoption."

"Why don't you get off the computer and help me pick up the house?"

"I don't like housework," I said. "Besides, information is power and I need to know more about this guy."

"Nobody likes housework." Carlos came over and leaned down to look at the screen. He smelled like raspberry yogurt and sex. Maybe the sex was my imagination.

"But I need to know about this guy. Maybe I can use it in court, or when Gabe and Freya go on about what a big help he is." I pressed some more keys.

Carlos took my hands and pulled me up from the seat. "Help me," he said.

"Help you what?" I put my arms around his neck and kissed him.

He lifted me up on the counter and stepped between my legs. "We were always good together."

His phone rang. "Ode to Joy."

"Don't answer it," I said. I put my hand inside his shirt. "We have better things to do."

I've almost got him convinced, but he leans over to see who's calling.

"I've got to take it," he said. "It's Chris's school."

Why does he have caller ID on Chris's school? I don't get much from his end of the conversation. Just a bunch of "yup" and "I understand."

He ended the call, put his phone in his pocket, and looked at me. "It seems you are getting into the wife part," he said. "You serious about being a mother?"

I nodded.

"Chris is in the principal's office for fighting. Want to come with me?"

"Yeah." It's what a mother would do.

The high school looked just like I'd remembered it. It's older than I am; red brick sprawled out over what used to be a horseracing track, back when tracks were dirt. I know that because my dad told me; he remembers when they built the school. Red brick, a white entrance canopy in front and a football field in back. It smelled the same too, like old paper and disinfectant.

We pressed a button to get in. That's new too; I guess security is tighter everywhere. The office, just to the right of the door, had glass all around it. We went up to a window and told them who we were. Must have been expecting us, because the principal came out and let us in himself.

"I'm Principal Hall." That's how he introduced himself, though I'm pretty sure his first name wasn't Principal. He was just a teacher when I attended this school. "I'm with the other student's parent right now; I'll be with you in a minute."

He pointed us to a small room where Chris sat alone, slouched against the wall.

"I told them not to call you." That's how he greeted us.

"What did you expect them to do?" asked Carlos. "They said you hit another kid."

"He deserved it." If anything, Chris slouched down lower.

I decided to let Carlos handle it, as I have no idea what to say.

"We only have a few minutes before we go into the office." Carlos went over and sat next to Chris. "Tell us what happened."

"It's not my fault," said Chris.

"Of course not," I agreed with him.

Carlos shot me a look. I sat down.

"Tell me."

Chris sat up straighter. "You won't believe me anyway."

"Try me," said Carlos.

"Randy was making fun of me, of Celeste, and of Mom." Chris stopped and stared at the wall, as if that explained everything.

"Go on," said Carlos.

"That's all." Chris slouched down again. "I had to stop him."

"By hitting him?" Carlos put his hand over Chris's hand.

I started to say something; then remembered I decided to let Carlos handle it.

"He was outside Grampa's house yesterday, making fun of Celeste. Called her retard and druggie. I told him to stop. He didn't."

"What happened today?"

"I was going to talk to him. Tell him to stop picking on Celeste." Chris had tears in his eyes.

I handed him a tissue.

"He said…he said…" Chris stopped talking.

"What did he say?" I asked.

"He said she was a retard, but that he'd had sex with her. That's all she's good for. Said she ran after him."

It took me a minute to figure out what he said. All his words jumbled together. He took a breath and kept on going.

"And he said I probably got some of the retard genes too. Said I probably had sex with my sister."

"And then you hit him." I wanted him to know it's okay to defend his sister.

"No, I didn't," Chris said. "He pushed past me and went to leave."

"When did you hit him?" This from Carlos.

Chris looked at me and then at the wall. He pulled his phone from his pocket. Carlos took the phone away from him.

"I didn't mean to," said Chris. "But he turned around and said I wasn't having sex with my sister because I was too busy having sex with my mother." He stared at me when he said it.

Principal Hall entered the room at that moment and we all went into his office.

"Chris was being bullied," I said. "You're supposed to do something about that."

"We can't do anything unless we know about it," said Principal Hall. "Why don't we all sit down and Chris can tell us what happened?"

We sat. Principal Hall behind his big-ass desk and us in chairs in front of him. This didn't bring back any good memories.

Hall looked at Chris. "Tell us what happened."

"Randy was making fun of my sister, Celeste. Called her a retard."

"Did he say anything else?" Hall asked.

Chris looked around the room.

"He said that Celeste and Chris were having sex and other nasty things about the family." If Chris wasn't going to say what happened, I would.

"I need Chris to tell me what happened," said Hall. "How did this incident start?"

"What you mean, how did it start?" Chris sat up straighter in his chair.

"Did Randy just come up to you and start yelling at you? Or did you seek him out?"

"Randy came up to Celeste yesterday and said nasty things to her." Chris sounded out of breath. "I went up to him today to tell him to knock it off."

"How many times has Randy said bad things to Celeste?" asked Hall.

"What's with all the questions?" I interrupted. "Don't you believe my son? Is it wrong to defend his sister? Or are you still taking your prejudices out against my family?"

"This incident has nothing to do with you." Hall leaned back in his chair.

Like hell it didn't. When I was in high school, I had an affair with my English III teacher. The teacher was fired, but the school tried to hush it up. I went to the local paper with my story. Hall was the head of the English Department and barely escaped with his job.

Carlos put his hand on my arm but didn't say anything to defend his son.

"Just trying to establish a timeline," said Hall. "If this is an incident of bullying, I want to know how long it's been going on."

That makes sense, so I don't say anything. I may have this mother thing down.

"Yesterday was the only time." Chris pulled out his phone. "I've got it on tape."

Chris turned the screen so we could all see. He'd recorded one minute and forty-three seconds of Randy calling Celeste "a retard" and her brother "a pervert" who had sex with her.

"See, it's not Chris's fault. The other kid was out of control." It felt good to defend my son. And to prove that Hall didn't know everything. I just wish Carlos would say something.

Chris put his phone back in his pocket.

"Did you record the beginning of the conversation?" asked Hall. "Did Randy just come up to your sister and start yelling?"

"No," said Chris. "But he was yelling at her afterward."

"Randy said that yesterday, he was riding his bike and your sister was standing in the middle of the bike path," said Hall.

"She didn't see him," Chris said. "He could've hit her."

"You were there?" At last, Carlos spoke.

"Yeah, I called Randy some names."

"According to Randy, Chris stepped out in front of him, causing him to go off the path, fall, and hurt himself." Principal Hall looked from Chris, to Carlos, to me.

"He only had some blood on his hands. And he was crying about dirt on his pants," said Chris. "He wasn't really hurt."

"If you had time to step out in front of Randy, he had time to avoid Celeste," said the principal.

I won't—can't—stay quiet any longer. "Chris was just defending his sister. That's a good thing to do."

"But this happened yesterday." Hall pointed his finger at me. "The fight was today, in school."

"Chris said the other kid was calling Celeste names and making fun of the family." I wondered why Carlos was so quiet; I needed help. "People have made fun of our family all my life. And you are out to get us. Maybe Chris just had enough of it." "There is no fighting in the school. Chris threw the first punch."

I stood up. "Chris is a good kid. People are always saying bad things about his sister." I leaned over the desk and got in Hall's face. "And about me. I'm sick of it and I'm sure Chris is too."

"Mrs. Leary, please sit down."

"It's Mrs. Vega. Carlos and I are married, long before Chris was born." I took a step closer to Hall's desk. "And I'm not going to sit down. Maybe I'll post this on social media and let everyone know how this school is run."

"I would advise against that," said Hall. "I have powerful friends and supporters."

I say some other things that Hall doesn't like. Chris is suspended three days for fighting. I have to call the school before I come in person. Carlos still doesn't say anything.

SATURDAY

MARCH 14, 2020

CHAPTER SIXTEEN

FREYA

"WE'RE SUPPOSED TO MEET CHLOE, FROM CITIZEN Advocacy, today." Gabe made this statement as he sat down at the table, early in the morning.

I was hoping I could drink my coffee in peace, before the girls woke up. "I know," is what I said.

Gabe added cream and three sugars to the coffee in front of him. "Do you want to meet with her?"

"Seems a little confusing to me," I said. "First, we have to meet with Richard Paoletti, who changed his name to Fontaine, then with this Chloe person. It's like the DCF runaround, a new person every week and whoever you're talking to doesn't know the answer to your questions."

Gabe stirred his coffee. "But Bonnie thinks she could help us."

"You just want to do what Bonnie says. You're smitten." This is a joke between us, the only time I ever use the word "smitten."

"There is that." As usual, he refused to argue about Bonnie.

"We could just talk to her; then decide," said Gabe. "It's not like we have to agree to everything, we can just get some more information."

"You always say that." I got up to get a second cup of coffee. "But you know that the more we talk to people, the more reason they have to be in our lives." I took a sip. Way too hot. "Like the DCF and people come see the girls; if we let them in, they'll find a reason to keep coming back."

"What you talking about?" Charity appeared in the doorway, dragging her blanket behind her. "Can I have breakfast?"

"Of course you can have breakfast." I pulled out a chair for her to sit in. "Where's Patrice?"

"She's jumping up and down in the crib." Charity looked at Gabe. "Can I have Cocoa Pops?"

"Sure," said Gabe at the same time that I said no.

Gabe looked at me. "I just think that we should meet with Chloe, take every chance we can get for help." He got up, went to the fridge, and got orange juice for Charity. "I'll make the cereal, you think about it."

"I better go see to Patrice before she jumps out of the crib." I went to leave the room.

"Do you want to help?" I assumed Gabe was talking to Charity.

I've got a bad feeling about my family. Not a specific fear, just a dark, heavy fog hanging over my family. My mother and grand-mother said the women in my family have a sixth sense and can tell things about people that other people don't notice. Sometimes it seems as if I know what people are going to say or do before they say or do it. Maybe I've just lived in this place with these people so long, I know them better than they know themselves.

I came back into the kitchen with Patrice.

"Bumpa left for work." This from five-year-old Charity, kneeling on her chair, something I've told her thousands of times not to do. "Can I have some more Cocoa Pops?"

I leaned over to look into the yellow and blue bowl before her. She slid her feet out from underneath her and sat in the chair. The bowl was empty. Celeste said that I shouldn't feed her Cocoa Pops. They're not real Cocoa Pops, anyway; they're the generic brand from the store. Celeste's not here today.

"How did you eat them so fast?" I asked Charity.

"I didn't eat them," she said. "Walter did."

I looked around that tiny kitchen. A stove, a refrigerator that needs to be wiped down as I see the fingerprints from here, and a wooden table with six chairs. I placed Patrice in the high chair next to me.

"I don't see Walter," I said.

Patrice smiled. I gave her a few dry Cocoa Pops on her tray. Celeste didn't tell me not to give them to her.

"That's 'cause Walter is my special friend. You can't see him." Charity put her spoon into the bowl. "And now we're both hungry."

"I didn't see Walter eat any food," I said. We play this game every morning. And sometimes at night, too. Bedtimes are something Walter tries to avoid.

"But he did and now I want some more."

I poured a half cup of cereal into her bowl. "If you eat this, you and Walter can have some more."

Charity took a spoonful. "Trice stinks," she said.

This is part of our morning routine, too. Patrice ate breakfast and then filled her diaper. I picked her up and went out into the hall to the changing table. I told Gabe it was much more practical to put the changing table in the great room where we eat and watch TV and spend most of our time. He insisted on putting it in the hallway.

I heard a knock on the door, a key turn in the lock, and then the wind moved down the hallway. It was so much more convenient when we could just leave the door unlocked, but at least our family has keys. Saved me from finding my third arm to hold Patrice, wrangle a diaper, and open the door.

"Hey, Gramma." Chris entered, followed by his father.

Charity ran past me and threw herself into Carlos's arms. "I'm ready to go, but Trice is stinky."

Carlos picked up Charity and swung her around.

"Be careful," I said. "She just ate." I finished diapering Patrice.

"Are you sure it's not a problem, taking both girls with you?" I hoped he wouldn't say that he'd changed his mind and it was a problem.

"Not at all." Carlos put Charity down. "Chris is taking a robotics class on Saturdays, out where the rich kids live." Carlos put his hand on Chris's shoulder. "When I found out there was an indoor kids' fountain and sprinkler nearby, I thought I'd take the girls and save myself driving out, then back, then out again to pick him up. We'll just spend the time getting wet."

"Charity has her bathing suit on under her clothes." I pulled up her shirt to show him. "Patrice needs special swimming diapers, and they're in the bag with extra diapers and a change of clothes. Charity's suit is from last year, but it still fits."

"Where's my mom?" asked Chris.

"She was in court yesterday." I put some crackers and cookies in the bag. The kids were always hungry after being in the water.

"She's supposed to be here."

It was the tone, not the words, that made me look at Chris. He wore a heavy silver ring on his right hand and he was spinning it around his finger. One of his tells when he's getting agitated or angry. I put both my hands around his.

"My mom said she'd come with us and fill out the emergency contact information for robotics classes." Chris pulled his hands away from mine.

"You can still go to camp," said Carlos. "I've given them my name and contact info and everything else is ready to go."

"That's not the point." Chris looked out the window. "She said she'd be here."

"Maybe she'll meet us at the school." Carlos picked up Patrice and the traveling bag.

He was lying to his child. He knew Jade wouldn't be there, just like I did. She didn't have a car and I knew of nobody to lend her one.

"Let's get going," I said. We picked up all the bags, toys, and clothes necessary to transport two preschoolers. Carlos was taking my car, with the car seats and the baby music, and leaving his for me, so at least we didn't have the mechanical rigmarole of transferring the seats. They left.

I went back into my suddenly quiet house. Last night, I'd made a list of all the things I'd do today with no kids for three hours. Now all I want to do is sit at the table and drink tea. The earlier feeling of dread returned. Maybe I shouldn't have let the kids go. It's hard to dwell on the negative when kids have to eat and talk and deal with invisible friends.

I decided to read the runes. Not just pulling a few runes, like I usually do, but laying them out in pattern and doing the divination. My grandmother called it divination, an attempt to reach and see the divine. Maybe I just like the feel of the stones in my hands. I picked up the bowls, spoons, cups, and cereal left over from the girls' breakfasts. I wiped down the table and the highchair, so I could start with a clean surface.

Taking down the velvet Crown Royal bag where I keep the runes, I noticed another box on the top shelf. Ignoring it, I opened the bag, took out the white silk cloth given to me by my grandmother. It's faded to yellow where it's been folded in the same way over the years. I spread it out over the table and sat down. Rather than just grab the runes from the bag, I spilled them all out on the table and turned them over, incised side down. Now, I can hover over the runes and pick out the ones I am attracted to for my layout.

Though I don't often choose a guiding rune or mentor rune, I felt the need to do so today. I touched and moved a dozen stones. The feel of the amethyst, cool and hard beneath my hand, soothed me. One rune sat far above the others, and I reached for it to bring it back down in front of me. I felt the cold as soon as I reached for it. Cold so intense I didn't want to touch the rune. It's already sixty-five degrees outside; all the runes are cool, but this one feels like dry ice. Gabe bought hamburg once, and it was delivered in dry ice. It hurt to touch it. I picked up the rune and put it in the upper right of the cloth, in the mentor position. It got warmer as I turned it over, as if it's satisfied that I've put it in the right place. Thorn, the rune of destruction. Not surprising, also the rune of the ice god. How did this come to be in the mentor position?

I touched it again. Still colder than the other runes, but not uncomfortable. Pictures flashed through my mind of breathless people, of closed and abandoned buildings, and of a gaping unknown. Not the destruction of my family, but of a wider destruction. This gives me some comfort, to know that my family might survive. But the dark unknown is still scary. Not sure I want to continue this rune pattern.

A rune fell off the table. I picked it up and placed it in the pattern, as the history rune. Othalan.

I looked at the runes for several minutes. Nothing came to me. Sometimes the runes don't want you to connect with the divine. I finished the pattern. Laguz was the foundation rune, the past of the family. It represented chaos. Yeah, we'd come from hard stock but we'd made it through. The aspiration rune was Feoh, for prosperity. That was a positive sign.

I heard the key turn in the lock and a pair of boots approached the table.

"Doing your witchery again?"

I stood up to face my husband. "Not again, still. I never stopped."

"Learn anything good?"

I scooped the runes into the bag. "They're not talking to me today." That was part of the truth. I didn't want to discuss the bad things I'd seen. "What are you doing home now? Aren't you working for Carlos today?"

"Do you believe that Stella was murdered?" Gabe asked the question as he sat down at the kitchen table. Hell of a conversation starter.

"I don't know. It seems possible."

"I don't know either." Gabe shook his head. "For the past few weeks, I've believed that Stella had a car accident. Just grateful that

Charity wasn't in the car with her. Thinking that it was deliberate makes me crazy."

Gabe always wanted to see the best in everyone. I knew there were evil people in the world. And people who just did stupid things, thinking they were helping.

"Why would someone want to kill Stella?" I asked. "She was only twenty-four years old; she didn't have time to do too many bad things in her life."

"Yeah, I always thought that Stella would make something out of herself. Graduated from high school with a scholarship, went to college for a while."

"Then she had to quit when she adopted Charity," I said. Gabe sometimes needed a reality check. Celeste's decisions and inability to raise Charity affected us all.

"But she was going back, she was going to finish." Gabe's firm belief that things would get better.

Gabe turned his mug in his hands and continued to stare. "Maybe Stella died because of something I did."

Gabe's other idea, that he was responsible for everything in the world. Not that he didn't cut corners and do some shady things, but he was basically a good man.

"What do you mean?" I couldn't imagine Gabe doing anything that would endanger his family.

"Maybe she saw something at the cobbler shop that she wasn't supposed to see. Maybe somebody was there who didn't know she was related to me and could keep her mouth shut. Maybe they thought she was Carlos's girlfriend and wanted to use her for leverage."

"That's ridiculous." I pushed the sugar over to Gabe's side of the table. "She's hung around the cobbler shop for years; everybody knows who she is. And she can't be leverage against Carlos if she's dead."

Gabe put sugar into his cup. "Maybe a warning to Carlos then. Not to mess around with the big guys. Now the police are investigating. Don't know if that's a good thing or a bad thing."

"I've got to put the runes away." I went to the pantry door to return the bag to the top shelf.

Gabe followed me. "I put Jade's box up on the top shelf the other day. Thought we might need it, now she's back."

I just stared at him.

"I haven't opened it yet," he continued. "Thought I might look at it now."

Jade's box contained her birth certificate; her childhood records, including school; her children's birth certificates; and her marriage certificate to Carlos. And a whole bunch of newspaper clippings. Gabe got the box down from the top shelf. It was shaped like a shoe box, though it was twice as big and made of sturdier material.

Gabe took the box down and I followed him into the kitchen. He put the box on the table, took off the top, and the yellowed newspaper clippings popped out onto the table.

We sat down at the table. The clippings weren't in any order, so I picked up the one nearest me. "Five-year-old left alone for four days," said the headline. I started reading out loud:

"Jade Leslie Leary, five years old, was left alone in her home for four days, in a snowstorm. She survived by eating snow, dry cereal, and uncooked macaroni. She was discovered by her grandmother when she couldn't get in touch with Jade's parents. Jade is the daughter of Michael Raphael Leary and Leslie (Canon) Leary, who were killed in a car accident."

"Stop," said Gabe.

"You still miss your brother." It wasn't a question. We put flowers on Mike and Leslie's grave every time we went to visit Stella in the cemetery. And, of course, Jade was a living symbol of her parents. She looked so much like Leslie.

Gabe and I were cross-country skiing in Canada during the incident, so I didn't have any firsthand knowledge. But I'd heard the story of how Gabe's mother, Marjorie, had got worried when she couldn't reach Jade and her parents in their cabin out in the woods.

She'd driven all night, through a snowstorm, to get there. Spent the last mile, on foot, with a flashlight, getting to the house. We could've lost her too.

Marjorie told that story many times. Last time was on her death-bed. Jade, who was a mother herself by that time, left the room.

"I don't know why I got that box down anyway," Gabe said. "Just bad memories."

"I know why you got it down." I rummaged through the box. "There are some good memories too."

I pulled out our wedding announcement, with Jade standing proudly between us. Both she and I were dressed in white, and she held a basket full of rose petals. "Jade was so happy to be our flower girl. She looked happy that day, though it was only a few months after her parents' deaths."

"Yeah, lots of people get married because there's a baby on the way." Gabe took the picture from me. "We got married to adopt a five-year-old."

"Oh, I was going to get you to marry me anyway." I took his hand. "Jade just sped up the process."

"We look so young." Gabe stared at the picture again. "Just twenty-one years old. We had no idea what was ahead of us."

"After forty years, you know me so well." He hugged me. "I'd marry you again, right now."

"Yeah, I love you too." I kissed him.

Then he deepened the kiss. I felt a familiar stirring. We didn't make love often but when we did it was always good.

I followed Gabe upstairs.

CHAPTER SEVENTEEN

GABE

Freya and i are going to meet with Chloe today. Though I talked Freya into the meeting, I'm beginning to have doubts about following through with this. Freya is right; every time we invite people into our house, we get more confusion and more people telling us what to do. Richard said that his people were different, but all the "helpers" say that. Well, we set up the meeting and it'd be impolite not to go. We agreed to meet at the Blind Pig, a local restaurant. Richard said that he would pick up the check, which is a good thing because Freya and I don't have the money to eat in a restaurant. We do takeout sometimes, but even that doesn't happen much.

Freya said we should dress nice to meet a new person. I didn't even know if I liked this new person. I wore my jeans and my boots. Freya did talk me into putting on my church shirt; white, and it buttoned up the front. Freya wore navy slacks and a blazer, with a lilac blouse underneath. I once called the blouse purple, but she informed me that it was lilac.

Richard and Chloe were at the restaurant when Freya and I arrived. They were in a back booth with high sides. That's good; it will let us talk without everybody hearing what we say. I didn't see Richard's scooter, but assumed it was around somewhere. Chloe stood up as we approached.

Chloe is just a tiny woman; she barely came to my shoulder. She has dark hair and stands like she has something she can't wait to tell you. She wore navy slacks and a blazer, and she had dog hair on her sleeve. She held out her hand and I took it.

"Chloe, this is Gabe and Freya," said Richard. "Gabe and Freya, this is Chloe Jay. She knows a lot about children and I'm hoping she can help you."

We all sat down. Richard and Freya on one side, Chloe and me on the other. There was some shuffling around and looking at each other.

Richard cleared his throat, like he was going to make a speech. "Gabe and Freya are raising their granddaughters, Charity and Patricia," he said.

"It's Patrice," said Freya. "And they are our great-granddaughters."

"Though we raised our granddaughters too." I don't know why I felt compelled to add that information.

"That seems to be happening more often," said Chloe. "Grandparents raising their grandchildren. But you are the first people I've met raising their great-grandchildren."

I felt like this was where we should tell them about why we ended up with the girls, but I wasn't ready for that discussion yet. Guess Freya wasn't either, because she kept her mouth shut.

The awkward silence was ended by the arrival of the waiter. He put little round pieces of paper in front of us and told us the day's specials.

None of us had looked at the menu, so we weren't ready to order. He took our drink orders: diet Cokes for me and Freya, a beer for Richard, and white wine for Chloe. Said he'd be back. Like that was a newsflash.

Richard tried again to get a conversation started. "Chloe is a school teacher," he said. "She knows a lot about child development and she used to be a truant officer, so she knows about the court system.

"They're called family liaisons these days, but truant officer will do."

I was liking this woman more.

"What were you hoping Chloe could help you with?" asked Richard.

"We're not sure she can." This from Freya, not showing any of the good manners she always talked to me about.

"We already have lots of people coming to the house to help us out," said Freya. "The DCF workers, early interventions for Patrice, and speech therapy for Charity. We have a lawyer and we're paying her for the custody case."

Chloe looked at Richard and Richard looked at Chloe.

Once again saved by the waiter, who set our drinks on the little round pieces of paper he'd left earlier. Once again, he asked for our order. Chloe and Freya ordered some special and Richard ordered a burger with mushrooms and cheese. That sounded good, so I had one too. The waiter left.

"Now, where were we?" asked Chloe. "Oh yes, why we might be able to help each other." She took a drink of her wine. "I'd be happy to talk about the girls, but I think we have some other things in common." She picked up her glass again, swirled the wine around inside, and put it back down. "I recently lost my partner. It was unexpected. My mother used to say that grief shared is grief halved. I'd like to find out if that's true."

I leaned back in the booth. I don't think I remember anyone ever sharing their personal life with us. Everyone said they were here to help but then they only talked about us and what they thought were our problems. Then I thought some more and looked over this big share of information. Maybe she was trying to get something from us, just going about it in a different way. Maybe I think too much.

"Is that why you want to visit us? For us to help you?" Freya asked.

Freya's voice sounded normal, but I know she can ask questions like she doesn't care about the answers. She gets lots of information that way. Sometimes I try to do it, but I'm not good at it like she is.

Richard started to say something, thought better of it, and shut up. This seemed to be a conversation between the women.

"No," said Chloe. "But I want you to know I'm not an expert, coming to lay knowledge on you. I know about children, but I don't know about your children. I know about grief and losing someone you care about, but I'm still learning about how to live with that. I want to help, but I'm not sure I can."

"Stella was murdered." Freya said that sentence without any emotion.

Chloe looked at Richard. "So was Jenna," she said. "You probably read about it; she was killed in the courthouse."

Some piece of information flitted around in my brain; then it was gone. "Seems like they have a problem with security in that courthouse."

"We're sorry that you lost someone, too," said Freya.

"Jenna worked in the courthouse for two years. I helped get her the job there." Chloe took a tissue out of her bag and wiped her eyes. "I'm sure you know how difficult it is."

The waiter arrived with the food. Freya wanted another Coke and Richard wanted mustard. A normal conversation about the food took a few minutes.

"You have a dog?" I asked Chloe.

She looked startled for a minute

"You have dog hair on your blazer," I said. "We weren't checking up on you." Though it was obvious that Chloe had checked up on us, else how would she know about Stella?

"Yes, Max, he's a mutt." Chloe brushed the hair off her sleeve. "Jenna and I rescued him about two years ago."

So, Jenna was her partner. Never met a woman with a female partner before. Except for the lady at the pharmacy with the short hair that stuck up straight and was dyed green.

"Do you have a dog?" she asked. She waved toward me. "No dog hair though."

"We sometimes take care of our grandson's dog, but we have no pets of our own." Freya's voice was getting more animated. Maybe she liked Chloe. "The children keep us busy, no time or energy for pets. Do you have children?"

Chloe didn't answer for several minutes. I got the idea that she didn't want to answer that question, though it was a normal one for Freya to ask.

"No, I don't have children." Chloe took a long swallow of her drink.

I was right, something about children upset her. Strange for a teacher. Maybe she had a bad experience recently. Freya seemed to sense that she was uncomfortable and didn't ask any more questions.

Chloe put her glass back on the table. "So, you have a court date coming up in the next few days. Do you want me to go to court with you? Offer moral support; maybe use my knowledge of the court to help you out?"

"That would be great," I said.

Freya glared at me. "I'd like to talk it over with our attorney," she said.

"I'll keep the date open," said Chloe. "I'll call you the night before and you can let me know what you decide."

The waiter came to clear the table. Nobody wanted dessert. I handed my plate to the waiter and it slipped. Mushrooms and beef juice ran all over my white Sunday shirt.

True to his word, Richard paid for the meal and he paid to have my shirt cleaned at the dry cleaner. First time the shirt got that treatment.

CHAPTER EIGHTEEN

GABE

I HURRIED FROM THE MEETING WITH CHLOE, AS I'D MADE an appointment to see Tina, Stella's friend. Freya had some errands to run and said she'd pick me up later. When I got to the diner, the place was almost deserted, now the dinner rush was over. A young couple was sitting in the back, both staring at their phones. A young boy, five or six, sat alone at the counter. He didn't have any food in front of him and he looked lost. Kids that young shouldn't be left alone.

Tina sat in a booth by the door. I slid into the vinyl seat across from her. "Thanks for agreeing to meet with me. Sorry I'm late."

"You said you'd buy me lunch," said Tina. "Had to eat anyway." She leaned back in the booth, and her faded dress stretched across her breast. She winked.

"I need to talk to you about Stella. I'm trying to figure out what happened to her."

"What do you want to know?"

I looked over at the counter. The young boy was still sitting there, banging his boots against the front of the counter. "How long has that boy been sitting there alone?" I asked.

"The boy at the counter?" asked Tina. "He's not doing anything."

"I know. But he's been sitting there alone. No adult in sight. Somebody could walk off with him, or hurt him."

Tina looked up and down the counter. "Maybe he's the kid of somebody who works here. Just waiting for his mom or dad. He's only been there a few minutes."

"That may be," I said. "But I'm going to make sure. Kids that young shouldn't be left alone."

I went over and sat down next to the kid. He looked at me when I said hello.

"I'm not supposed to talk to strangers," he said.

"That's a good thing to remember," I said. "My name's Gabe. What's yours?"

"Tommy."

"Now we're not strangers. What you doing here Tommy?"

"Waiting." He grabbed the salt and pepper shakers from the basket and started playing with them.

"Your parents work here?" I asked.

A woman in a wool coat and a fur hat came up to us. "Who are you talking to, Tommy?"

"Aunt Sue, this is Gabe." Tommy gestured in my general direction.

"You know you're not supposed to talk to strangers," said Aunt Sue. She turned to me. She smelled like Chanel No. 5; my mother used to use that fragrance. "What do you want with my nephew?"

"I just saw him sitting here alone. Wanted to make sure he was okay."

"How do I know that?" asked Sue. "You could take him away with you or hurt him."

"My point exactly," I said. "It's dangerous to leave a child that young by himself. You should stay with him at all times."

"Not that it's any of your business, but he didn't want to stay in the ladies' room. I take good care of him."

"But he's so young. You need to watch him."

Aunt Sue pulled Tommy off the stool. "What I need is for you to stop telling me what to do with my nephew, who you never met before today." She took a step toward the door. "Come along Tommy." She dragged him by the arm and they left the diner.

I sat back down, across from Tina. The waitress came over with white ceramic cups and a carafe.

"Coffee?" she asked.

I nodded. I felt the heat as she filled up my cup. She plunked the cup in front of Tina and filled hers. I wasn't hungry but didn't want to sit here without buying anything. The diner was run by a local man and hadn't changed much in forty years. I wondered how he kept it going.

"Good for you," said the waitress, leaning toward me. "Somebody needs to watch out for kids these days. No matter what that woman said."

"I know. Kids can get into trouble so fast."

"Ain't that the truth. By the way, my name's Nancy. I'll be back in a few to get your orders." She left.

"Why'd you do that?" asked Tina.

"Do what?"

"Go talk to that kid." Tina took a sip of coffee. "That's a dangerous thing to do these days. People'll think you're a pervert."

"I did get yelled at." I looked at Tina, in her too-tight dress and her plastic earrings. "But it's important that kids not get left alone. Stella's mother, Jade, was left alone as a child and it's affected her whole life."

"What happened?" asked Tina.

"I don't want to talk about it now." I stared into the coffee cup. "I want to talk about Stella. I don't know much about what she did outside the house, so I thought I'd talk to you."

Tina looked at me. "Why now?" I heard the red vinyl seat creak as she settled into it.

"The police think it may not have been an accident," I said.

The waitress came back to take our order. I ordered a corn muffin. Tina ordered a Caesar salad.

"That all, hon?" The waitress waited with her pencil poised over her pad.

"Bring me some rolls and butter, please." Tina glanced at the menu again.

"Coming right up." She left again.

"So, what can you tell me about Stella?" I asked.

"Yeah, me and Stella were buds since second grade. And Danny, too."

"I thought you met Danielle in high school. I don't remember hearing about her before then."

"Yeah, Danny started school with us; then moved away. She came back when she was in high school and we were the three musketeers."

"Which one was D'Artagnan?" I asked.

"Who?"

Guess she'd never read the book and maybe didn't know what a musketeer was.

"Never mind." I took a sip of my coffee.

"What happened to Stella, then?" Tina asked. "Do they think it was suicide?"

"Suicide? Why would you say that?"

"You said that it wasn't an accident. I can't see Stella doing suicide, though."

I'd never considered that possibility. The thought that bright, happy Stella, with a young child to raise, would take her own life.

The waitress interrupted my thoughts. She placed the salad, piled high on a dinner plate, and the rolls on the table.

"Anything else you need?" she asked. The diner was due to close soon and I wondered if she wanted us to leave.

"I'm fine," I said.

Tina stared at her salad. "Can I get some French fries? And a diet Coke?" she asked.

"Be right back," said the waitress.

"I need food if we're going to talk about suicide." Tina picked up a roll and smeared butter over the surface. "How come they say that the accident is still under investigation?"

"Who's they?"

"Her friends, the police. It's all over Facebook and Instagram."

I had only a vague idea what Instagram was, though I watched television, where everybody was complaining about Facebook and elections.

Nothing like the direct approach. "The police came to talk to Freya and me. They think that Stella may have been murdered."

Tina put down her fork. "Murdered? Who would want to kill Stella?"

"That's what I'm trying to find out. Asking questions of her friends."

"No, Stella was going through some hard times. But she didn't kill herself and nobody else did it either."

Tina sounded so sure, but I had my doubts. "How do you know that?"

Tina picked up her fork, took a bite of her salad, and looked out the window. "This salad is pretty good." She took another bite. "But not as good as the French fries here."

I jumped when somebody in the kitchen dropped some flatware. A lot of flatware. There was a pass-through to the dining area and everybody heard it.

"Happens all the time, the dishwasher's a klutz." The waitress came up to the table with a coffee pot. "Refill?"

I looked down at my cup. It was empty. I pushed it in her direction and she filled the cup.

"I'd like a diet Coke," said Tina.

"I'll bring it out with your fries." The waitress left.

"What's this about Stella going through hard times?" I asked.

"You know," said Tina. She moved lettuce around her plate. "It was stressful, making all the plans to move her and Charity."

"Move Charity?"

Tina looked up at me. I guess I said it louder than I thought.

"Yeah, you know, to Boston." Tina became very interested in her food.

I didn't say anything.

"Stella wanted to go to school," Tina said. "She was filling out applications, and trying for money to help her out. Then she got some money from her stepdad, Carlos."

"I saw the forms around the house. Lent her money for some application fees." This had been last summer, when she applied to the local community college, and I hadn't seen the papers or lent her money since.

"Didn't you know? She got into the nursing program at Simmons," Tina said. "Planned to start there next September."

I leaned back in the booth. "What was she going to do with Charity?"

"Take her with her," said Tina. "You know, when she moved to Boston."

Stella was planning to move to Boston? With Charity? Why didn't I know about this?

The waitress set the fries and a diet Coke in front of Tina. This meeting was going to cost me more than I planned. I didn't have any money and neither did Stella. She could never finance such a move.

Tina must have picked up on my confusion.

"Maybe she meant to tell you, but she died first. She'd just told us she got accepted and we were planning what to do next."

"What do you mean, 'we were planning what to do next'?" Tina took a fry and bit into it. Stared out the window. "We had a plan. We were all going to move to Boston, rent an apartment together," she said. She took another fry. "I'm a pharmacy tech, I can work anywhere. Stella was going to school and maybe waitress on the weekends. Danielle wasn't sure what she was going to do, 'cause her boyfriend wanted to go with her."

"Her boyfriend?" I'm not sure why I thought that was a relevant issue.

"Yeah, her boyfriend Ben. He wants her to stay here, marry him, and have a bunch of kids. Or he'd go to Boston with her. Don't think that's what she wanted to do."

The waitress came over. "Do you want anything else?" she asked.

"I think I'll have a piece of blueberry pie," said Tina. "With ice cream. And another diet Coke."

I ordered a refill on my coffee and watched the waitress walk away. The waitress kept coming over; maybe she wanted us to finish up so she could leave. I can probably put this on my credit card. I'm *just* below the credit limit, but this shouldn't be a problem.

Something shook loose in the back of my mind. "Didn't Stella have a boyfriend? Back in the fall. She introduced me to your brother, Adam. Said they were a couple."

Tina waved her hand. "That was months ago. It's over and Stella was going with us."

The waitress put the pie and the diet Coke in front of Tina, filled my coffee cup, and left the check.

"How was Stella going to pay for school and an apartment?"

"She got money from Carlos. Lots of money." Tina took a bite of pie. "Guess Carlos is her stepdad, but he gave her thousands of dollars."

"Loan or gift?" I asked.

Tina shrugged. "Don't know what we're going to do now," she said. "Stella's dead and Danielle's probably going to marry Ben." She picked up a napkin to wipe tears from her eyes.

Don't know whether she's crying for Stella or for her lost opportunities.

"What about your brother?" I asked. "How'd he take the breakup? He just seemed to disappear one day."

"My brother wouldn't do nothing to hurt Stella." Tina put down her fork. "He was shook up, but now he's got a new girlfriend."

"Why did Stella borrow all that money from Carlos? How was she going to pay it back?"

"Don't know what her agreement was with Carlos," said Tina. "But, according to Stella, he had lots of money."

I thought about Antonio, the last person who was slow to pay Carlos back.

Tina put down her fork. "According to local postings, you didn't want Stella to leave."

For a moment, I thought someone had posted flyers on telephone poles. Then I realized she was talking about stuff on the computer. "I didn't want Stella to leave," I said. "But I didn't kill her."

"Neither did I," said Tina. "Just telling you what the gossip is."

Another piece dropped into place. If she'd seen it on the computer, Tina knew all along that I was someone they suspected. Maybe she was trying to get information from me. Tina continued to scarf down her pie.

I didn't like this. I got up, paid the bill at the counter with my credit card. It cleared and I left.

CHAPTER NINETEEN

GABE

FREYA PICKED ME UP FROM THE DINER, WE PICKED UP THE kids, and I dropped everybody off at home. One more stop for me. I had to go talk to Carlos. I went to the cobbler shop. He was in the front with Jade when I walked in. They stopped talking and backed away from each other. Not my issue.

"Carlos, I need to talk to you," I said.

"You can talk in front of me. Carlos has no secrets," said Jade.

"This has to do with Carlos, not you." I put my messenger bag on the counter. "It's about the business."

"Sure it is." Jade picked up her purse, yanked open the door, and left.

"You want to talk about Jade?" asked Carlos.

"No," I said. "I want to talk about Stella."

Carlos raised his eyebrows, as if he didn't believe me, but he sat down. "Stella? What about Stella?"

"I just had a meeting with Stella's friend, Tina."

"The short girl, likes older men?"

I don't want to know how Carlos got that information. "Yes. She told me you gave Stella a lot of money, just before she died."

"Yeah, she wanted money for school, so I gave her some," said Carlos. "We had a good year; it wasn't a problem."

"Why didn't you tell me?"

"I'm her stepfather. I can give her money if I want to."

"She lived with me. I should've known if she was planning to leave."

Carlos slammed his hand on the counter. "Why does this matter now? Stella's dead and she won't be spending the money."

"That's the problem, isn't it?" I leaned across the counter. "Working for you seems to have more problems than solutions. I'm considering laying low, not working until this custody thing works out."

"Don't think it's anything to worry about," he said. "I contribute to cop charities and spread money around so they don't bother me. The assistant chief occasionally places a bet with me. Working for me shouldn't be a problem."

I knew that, but was still uneasy. "But I don't want them looking into my life, with my disability and the girls living with us." I stopped talking when I realized that Carlos might not have the same interests that I did. It's getting too confusing. "Maybe I should stop working for you for a while. Just for a few weeks." It had to be just a few weeks, or our bills wouldn't get paid.

Carlos stared out the window. I turned around to look, but didn't see anything interesting out there. When I turned back, Carlos had a paper bag in his hand.

"Just one more run," he said. "Les at the hardware store wants his winnings. They haven't stopped you there, have they?"

I shook my head. "By the time I get there, Les will have thought of some other bets he wants to place, and I'll end up bringing the money back anyway." It had happened several times.

"Yeah, but he's a good customer, pays regular, and we need to keep him happy." Carlos handed me the paper bag. "I need to keep on his good side, because he's a selectman. I'll pay you double if you do it right now."

I put the money in my messenger bag and went out. Just one more delivery. I parked on the street and got out of the car. A parking meter monitor was standing on the sidewalk, so I dug change out of my pocket. This was my last run and I didn't want to draw attention to it. I looked at the parking monitor again. He seemed a little old for the job, in his forties, and had the build of a bouncer, complete with sunglasses. The job didn't pay well, and people got yelled at a lot, so most of the parking people were young kids. I hoped I wasn't going to be hassled about parking again.

"Sir, you can't park there," he said.

"I'll just be a few minutes," I said. "Got a delivery for Les." I made a show of putting the coins in the meter.

I saw myself reflected in his sunglasses. In March, he's wearing sunglasses. In New England, where it'll be dark soon.

"Are you Jesus Gabriel Leary?" He pronounced my name the correct way, "hey-soos."

"Yeah. Can I park here now?"

"Mr. Leary, you are under arrest." While he said this, he pushed me up against my car, twisted my hands behind my back, and handcuffed me. The shoulder I'd injured felt like dozens of needles were going through it.

"Hey, I got an injured shoulder."

"Then I'll take this." A second man, tall and skinny, in uniform complete with gun belt, had my message bag. With the $820 for Les in it.

"Don't struggle and you'll be fine," said the first cop, as he dropped his vest with "Parking" across the back on the hood of my car. He took my arm and walked me toward the cruiser that must have arrived with the second cop.

"What's the charge? Illegal parking?" I'm not usually sarcastic to authority, but I couldn't figure out what I did wrong.

"Assault and battery." Couldn't tell which cop said it.

"Assault and battery of who? I just parked my car."

"Of Jade Vega," said the skinny cop. "She filed a complaint this morning."

I shut up. Afraid another charge would be added when they searched my bag.

CHAPTER TWENTY

GABE

THEY TOOK ME TO THE POLICE STATION. THIS MUST BE serious. Few times I was arrested before, when I was young and stupid, they just took my name and issued a summons. They asked me identifying information that they could've got off my driver's license and fingerprinted me. They put me into a small room with a table, welded to the floor, and three metal chairs. I sat there for over an hour. Guess they wanted me to think about my wicked ways.

The door opened and the cop that pretended to be a parking monitor entered the room, followed by somebody I didn't recognize. Both now wore ties and had on jackets. The guy who arrested me seemed to be in charge; he was at least twenty years older and forty pounds heavier than his counterpart. The younger guy obviously took better care of himself and his suit fit better.

"I'm Detective Robichaud." The older cop sat down across from me. "And this is Detective Landers."

The younger cop remained standing, but leaned against the wall.

"Why am I here?" I asked. "And when do I get my phone call?"

"We need to talk to you about the assault charge." Robichaud opened the file he'd brought in with him. "And about the eight hundred and twenty dollars we found when we arrested you."

I wasn't sure Robichaud knew where the money came from or

was going to, but Carlos was clear on what to do in this situation. "I want a lawyer."

Landers stood up straight. "It will go easier on you if you talk to us. If we book you, you'll be in the system for a while and I don't think you want that."

Guess Landers was the good cop, so I addressed myself to Robichaud. "I want a lawyer."

Robichaud took a piece of paper out of his file and put it in front of me. "Acknowledgment of Miranda Warnings" was displayed in bold letters across the top,

"Will you sign your Miranda warnings?" asked Robichaud. "You have the right to remain silent." He went through the rest of the warnings.

I signed the paper, as Carlos told me to do. Didn't want anybody to think I was uncooperative, though that's what I intended to be.

Landers walked the few steps from the wall to the end of the table. "You don't have to talk to us, but I want to point out some things to you. Your daughter is pressing assault charges against you. I understand that's a domestic thing and not our area of expertise anyway."

I don't trust a cop that uses phrases like "area of expertise." Though it did get me wondering what his expertise was. I didn't have to wait long.

"As a detective, I work on organized crime and gambling," Landers continued. "I was called in today because we know you work for Carlos Vega, as a runner. If you flip on him, we can make this all go away."

I stared at Landers, then Robichaud. Carlos was family and I wasn't saying anything.

They took me out of the room, let me call Freya, and put me into a holding cell with one other person, who was sleeping on the bench and smelled of urine and cheap booze. It wasn't until I was in the cell that I realized they didn't ask me anything about Stella and her death.

CHAPTER TWENTY-ONE

FREYA

THE CALL CAME FROM GABE ABOUT THREE HOURS AFTER he left. I was worried, didn't know where he was. He said he was at the police station, had been arrested because Jade filed charges.

Didn't want to talk about it, because the cop was standing right there. They added other charges when they saw what was in his bag. I needed to call Carlos.

A second after I hung up, I heard Patrice cry. The noise then woke up Charity. So much for their naps.

I got Charity to the bathroom, changed Patrice's diaper, and started downstairs. Both girls would be needing a snack but first I needed to call Carlos. He answered immediately and I conveyed Gabe's message.

"How long ago did they take him?" asked Carlos.

"Don't know, but he's been gone about three hours. Last I saw him, he was on his way to see you. Now he's at the Meredith police station."

"I've got a bail bondsman on call. I'll have him out by tomorrow at the latest."

"Tomorrow? You mean he needs to spend the night in jail?"

"It's Saturday," said Carlos. "But I'll do my best." He hung up without saying goodbye.

I got both girls settled at the table, put bowls of Cheerios in front of them (no milk for Patrice), and poured the orange juice. I was handing Charity a spoon when I heard pounding on the door.

"Open up. Police."

It was like a bad dream that wouldn't end. I went to open the door.

"You already took my husband," I said, wanting to get in the first word.

"Yes, ma'am, we're here to serve a search warrant." The thin man in a uniform waved a piece of paper in front of my face. "Is there anybody in the house besides you?"

"My great-grandchildren are here. They're in the kitchen eating."

"Don't tell them anything else, Freya." This statement was from Carlos, who must have broken some speed limits getting here.

"Sir, who are you?" asked the police officer with the warrant.

"I'm Carlos Vega. I'm Freya's son-in-law."

"He can't go in." This from a man in a suit standing in my yard. He didn't have a uniform, but he stood like a police officer. "He may be involved in this matter."

Carlos started to argue with the man in the suit. I went back into the house to tend to the girls. The uniformed police officer followed me in.

"Ma'am, I'm asking that you and the children remain seated at the table while we search."

There were now several officers going through my house. Carlos never did get in. The girls finished their snack and the uniformed officer—he said to call him Bill—took the dishes to the sink.

We sat at the table until the girls started to whine. I got up to get something for them to do.

Bill stood up also and blocked my way. "Ma'am, please remain seated at the table."

"Can't," I said. "Unless they have something to do, these girls are going to turn into screaming meanies. I need to go get them some toys."

Bill adjusted his belt and threw his shoulders back. "Ma'am, you need to stay here. I'll have some toys brought in."

Bill went to the door and called over another cop, asked him to get some things for the kids to play with. Never left the room, like we were going to escape if he stepped outside. Thought had crossed my mind, but I'd have problems running and carrying the kids at the same time.

Another cop delivered paper, crayons, and a deck of cards to the table. We drew pictures of dogs, and unicorns, and houses. Then we played slapjack. Patrice wasn't very good at it, except for the slapping part, but it passed the time.

The cops went through the entire house. They opened the storage containers in the basement and went through the girls' toys. Every bed was stripped and the mattresses turned. They even checked behind where the paneling was coming loose in the back room. They dumped out my runes and the box full of Jade's mementos on the counter and left them there. The large cop wouldn't even let me get up from the table to pick them up.

I'd finally had enough of this. Patrice was fussing, so I took her with me to find the cops in the living room.

"Ma'am, you can't come in here." A uniform blocked my way.

"It's my house," I said. "The kids are tired and they need to go to bed. What do you want me to do?"

"Go back into the kitchen," said the uniform. "I'll see what I can do."

We played three more games of slapjack, but we were all getting bored with it.

The uniform came into the kitchen with a female cop.

"We've cleared upstairs," he said. "You can go up there with the girls, but you'll have to stay there. Officer Kelly will need to search you and the girls first."

Seemed like the only way we were getting upstairs, so I agreed. The female cop undressed both girls and even checked inside Patrice's diaper. She patted me down and made me take the used Kleenex and old shopping list out of my pocket. She also inspected the crackers and cheese I took upstairs to feed the girls before they went to bed.

Once we got upstairs, the girls were so overtired and cranky that it took a while to settle them down. The food helped; you could see Charity relax as she ate. Finally, both girls were in bed. I went to sit in the rocking chair in our room. The police were still banging around downstairs, taking out the plumbing for all I knew. It was after ten that night before Officer Kelly came to tell me they were leaving. I followed her downstairs and locked the house after her. Then I started picking up the toys and papers and general mess left by the police. They made no effort to clean up anything

It was after midnight when I finally quit. Gabe wasn't coming home tonight.

SUNDAY

MARCH 15, 2020

CHAPTER TWENTY-TWO

JADE

I NEEDED HELP TO GET CUSTODY OF THE GIRLS AND I MIGHT need some help in parenting. My Dad was in jail, my fault, and I needed to get him out. Carlos can help with all these things. I dressed to impress and went to see him.

Carlos sat in the cobbler shop, behind the counter that goes along the back wall. He looked up when I came in and his eyes followed me across the floor. Two seconds on my face, thirty seconds on my body, thirty seconds on my shoes. My shoes were impressive. High heels with leather laces.

"You look good," he said.

Not "How have you been?" or "Hello." Just a comment on my appearance.

"You look pretty good yourself."

He continued to stare. He's a very good cobbler and excellent working with his hands.

I stood there, one foot in front of the other. My legs are my best feature, according to Carlos. I like my hair better; it's long and black and I could do a head sweep to kill for.

"You looking for sex?" Carlos smiled.

Just like him to go there first. But, hey, I'm forty years old and still have it. Okay, so I'm over forty, but I pass for thirty in dim light.

"What makes you think I want to have sex with you?" I'm curious.

"Darling, we've always been good together." He put down the boot, sauntered over to me, and ran his fingers up my arm.

"We have, haven't we?" I smiled. Some of the old feeling was coming back. He smelled like cigarettes and leather with an undertone of lemon. And his fingers were now going down the front of my shirt. They stopped at my breast.

"So, what do you want?" he asked.

I kissed him. A full-frontal, tongue-down-the-throat kiss. He's interested.

He stepped back. "We going to have sex here on the shoes?" he asked.

I looked around at the plate glass window, showing the street outside, and the long counter in full view of the front door. "I'm game if you are," I said.

"Always the exhibitionist." Carlos shook his head. "What is it you want?"

It looked like the discussion needed to take place now. "My dad's in jail."

Carlos nodded. Of course, he knew that.

"Mom's freaking out," I continued. "And I need to get Dad out of jail. His bail is two thousand and I don't have it."

Carlos stepped in closer. "And how're you going to pay me back?"

"I got a job. At Dunkin Donuts." Well, I'd applied for a job there.

"If you've got a job, why don't you pay his bail?" Carlos picked up a strand of my hair and wound it around his finger.

"I just started." Well, I was going to start as soon as they called me. "I don't have two thousand dollars. And you can make that back in a day."

"And what about the vig?"

I'd been around Carlos long enough to know that the "vig" is the amount the bookmaker charges in interest. And it's usually quite a bit.

"We can discuss the vig," I said. I stepped closer to him and touched him where he's hard.

He put the "Closed" sign on the door and we went upstairs to his apartment.

Sex with Carlos was always interesting. He had silk scarves, sex toys, and fuzzy handcuffs. Not that he wasn't considerate. I totally relaxed and fell asleep when we finished.

I woke about an hour later with Carlos leaning on his elbow and looking down on me. He pinched my nipple as I opened my eyes.

"I have to go open the shop," he said.

"It could wait a few more minutes." I pulled him down toward me.

I didn't get off that second time, but he seemed to enjoy it. Afterward, he sat on the edge of the bed to put on his pants.

I ran my finger down his back. "So, are you going to put up the money to bail out my dad? It's two thousand dollars, cash bail."

He took my hand and kissed it. "It's *one* thousand dollars, cash bail," he said. "And my bail bondsman made arrangements to pay it a few hours ago."

Shit, I was hoping I could get some spending money out of this. "You had sex with me, after you'd already done what I asked?"

Carlos stood up and pulled on his pants. "I have a bail bondsman on standby." He buttoned his fly. "And what were you going to do with the other thousand?"

Busted. "I need some spending money. I haven't got paid at my job yet."

"Do you even have a job? How are you going to pay me back?"

I sat up in bed and pushed the covers aside. Let him see what I'm offering. "No, but I may have a job soon. And look what you're getting in the meantime."

He looked me over from head to toe. He picked up his shoes and his shirt and went into the bathroom.

I figured I would leave while the leaving was good. I threw on my clothes and ran down the back stairs to the parking lot.

And directly into my father, who was getting out of his car.

CHAPTER TWENTY-THREE

JADE

Hᴇ ʟᴏᴏᴋᴇᴅ ᴍᴇ ᴏᴠᴇʀ. I ᴅɪᴅɴ'ᴛ ᴘᴜᴛ ᴏɴ ᴍʏ ꜱᴛᴏᴄᴋɪɴɢꜱ; they were bunched in my hand. My hair was a mess and I felt whisker burn on my cheeks. And I smelled like Carlos's cigarettes.

My father walked toward me. "I guess I don't have to ask what you've been doing."

"I did it for you." The words came out before I could stop them.

"You slept with Carlos for me? What do I get out of that deal?"

I stuffed my stockings in my purse. Didn't need them anyway. "I needed to get you out of jail," I said.

"Carlos has people for that." My dad sounded disappointed.

"Yeah, he told me that." I waved my hand. "After, you know."

"So, you slept with Carlos to get me out of jail? Rather than going to your mother and helping her with the grandkids? She's taking care of them alone."

"What are you doing here, instead of going home to help her?" Bet he didn't have a good answer for that.

"I'm doing the polite thing. I came to thank Carlos for bailing me out; then I'll go home and help your mother."

I didn't get to answer him, because Carlos came to the door to turn around the sign. As soon as it said "Open," my dad started over there.

Dad took only a few steps then turned around to face me again. "Jade, please go home and help your mother. Tell her I'll be there as soon as I can." He gave me a five-dollar bill. "This is for bus fare."

Five bucks. What does he expect me to do with five bucks? It takes a dollar to get to my mother's house and another dollar to get to my house. Not even enough left over for a drink at Starbucks. As if this town had a Starbucks.

I started walking. I'd gone only about a block when a car pulled up beside me. It's an old junker, but the driver was hot. Larry Lapinski, a flame of my daughter, Celeste.

Larry leaned over and opened the passenger door. "Hey, Mrs. V., you want a ride?"

Beat walking. I climbed into the car. "You can call me Jade."

The passenger seat was relatively clean, but litter covered the floor: fast food wrappers and discarded cigarette packages. The car smelled like Marlboros. Carlos's brand and the choice of Larry also, to judge by the stuff on the floor. Though it appeared that he smoked a generic brand also, maybe when money was tight.

"Where you going?" he asked.

I thought about it for thirty seconds. Gabe was going home after he talked to Carlos, so there's no hurry to get to my mother. She's taken care of kids for years; she's good at it. "Nowhere in particular. Where are you going?"

"I'm on my way to pick up Celeste," he said. "She's at the suboxone clinic."

"Suboxone?" I asked. "She's trying to kick her habit?"

"Yeah, I told her the heroin's making her old. She needs to cut down. Stick to cocaine and meth."

I looked at him. He'd lost about twenty pounds since I last saw him.

"Meth?" I said. "You still cooking it at the trailer?"

"Yeah, it's an easy way to make money. And I'm good at chemistry. Celeste is good at selling, so we do okay."

He pulled up in front of a plain cement block building. Celeste was sitting on the front steps. She came over to the car.

"What's she doing here?" Celeste's question was aimed at Larry.

"I picked her up as she was walking home." He kissed Celeste. "Is that a problem?"

"Guess not." She opened the door and got into the back seat. "Doctor didn't make it in today. I've got to go to his office to pick up my script."

"No problem." Larry turned the car around and headed back the way we came.

Just as I was ready to make some remark about not wanting to go back to where I started, he pulled into a parking lot.

Celeste leaned forward between the seats. "Don't know how long this will take me. Do you want to come in or wait in the car?"

"I need to pick up some things at Walmart," said Larry. "I'll go while you're in there and pick you up when I'm finished."

"Okay," said Celeste. "You coming in with me, Ma?"

"No, I think I'll go to Walmart, pick up some things." Not that my five bucks would get me far.

"See you soon." Celeste disappeared into the office building.

"What do you need to pick up at the store?" asked Larry.

"Some food, clothes." I had an idea. "New underwear. The stuff I've got on is old." I unzipped my pants and showed him my black thong. "See how stretched out it is." I pulled the back down and showed him the little triangle in the back.

"Can I help you pick out your new underwear when we get to the store?"

"You could," I said. "But it's just a dream. I don't have enough money to buy new underwear."

"I could help you with that." He put the car in gear with more force than was necessary.

"I'd be so happy if you could give some money." I put my hand on his thigh. It flexed as he drove.

We reached the parking lot in record time and Larry pulled into a space far from the main entrance.

"How much money do you need?" he asked.

"Two hundred dollars should do it." I inched my hand further up his thigh.

"Two hundred bucks? For underwear? At Walmart?" He turned off the car and faced me. "I don't have that much money."

We went back and forth for a few minutes and settled on $115. That included forty-five in cash that he had in his wallet; he'd charge the rest.

"Thank you for the money," I said.

"Show me how thankful you are."

He's young and not very subtle. But he was cute and clean. I pulled down his pants and showed him how grateful I was, right there in the back of the parking lot.

We went into the store. He bought motor oil and a funnel to put it into the car. I picked up bread, cheese, and bananas. As I was going to show up late at my mother's house, I also got chocolate cookies for the kids.

Larry and I went to the women's lingerie section. Larry wanted me to buy another black lace number, but I wanted something different. We settled on an orange set with flames in strategic places. Larry wanted me to try it on, but the clerk in the ladies' fitting room was a jerk about it.

Larry and I went back out to the car and picked up Celeste. She was in a pissy mood, said she'd been waiting almost twenty minutes.

"I want to sit in front with Larry," said Celeste. "Ma, get in the back."

I didn't want to fight with her so I got in the back.

Celeste picked up the Walmart bag from the floor in the front seat, where I left it.

"What did you buy at Walmart?" she asked.

She opened the bag and took out the orange thong with flames on it.

"You make me wait to buy this?" Celeste said. "What do you need this for?"

"I needed new underwear," I said.

"And this is what you need?" Celeste held the thong with her middle finger.

I think I heard Larry laugh.

I needed to leave this situation. "Larry, will you drop me off at my mother's house? I promised Dad I would check on Mom and the kids."

"What's wrong with Mom and the kids?" Celeste did not seem at all interested.

"Dad got arrested today. Working for Carlos."

"Is he in jail?"

"He had a thousand dollars cash bail."

"I could bail him out," said Celeste. "I had good sales today." She took out a wad of cash, two inches thick, with a fifty-dollar bill on top.

I took the wrong person shopping with me.

"The bail has to be paid in full. One thousand."

Celeste counted out twenty fifty-dollar bills and handed them to me.

I counted them again. "Sure this won't make you short?" I asked.

"No, we're ahead," said Celeste. "Larry is a good chemist. We've paid off our suppliers and we still have money left, now that I'm not using as often. Besides, it's Dad."

Larry looked like he was going to say something but changed his mind at the last minute.

We approached my parents' house and I hoped that Dad wasn't standing out front, blowing my story about him needing bail. Not that I said he still needed bail; that was just what Celeste thought. The coast was clear, not even Dad's car made it home yet.

"Thanks." I hopped out of the back seat with the groceries in my arms. Celeste handed me the other bag through the front window. "I'm sure Dad will be happy to see the bail money."

I walked into chaos. Patrice had taken off her diaper and was chasing Charity and hitting her with it. I saw Chris's Siberian husky come up and knock Patrice off her feet. She started to cry. Blocks and trucks and blankets were scattered on the floor. I picked up Patrice, put her diaper back on, and sat her on the couch. Charity climbed up beside her and I gave cookies to both girls. I pushed the dog away from the girls and their cookies and he laid down on one of the blankets. It had yellow ducks and blue fish on it, so it probably wasn't his blanket, but at least it's quiet.

"What's going on in here?" My mother entered the room, still holding a wooden spoon she used for making soup. "Oh, Jade, Gabe called an hour ago and said you were coming right over."

"I got held up," I said. "But I'm here now."

"Are you feeding the girls cookies? Supper's almost ready, you'll spoil their appetite."

No acknowledgement that I didn't have to be here and I'd got both kids and the dog to be quiet. Sometimes my mother doesn't appreciate everything I do.

Charity went over to the bag and took another cookie and my new underwear. My mother grabbed the cookie from Charity, stuffed the underwear into the bag, and handed it to me. I'm glad I put the money into my purse and she didn't see that.

Charity started to scream again, now that she'd finished her cookie. She tried to take the other cookie from Patrice, who started screeching also. I'd got everybody calmed down and, in a few minutes, my mother had created chaos again. She's good at doing that. All she needed was to read her runes and make some dire predictions to make my miserable day complete.

The smoke alarm went off in the kitchen.

"Oh, dinner will be ruined." My mother left the room.

I gave Charity and Patrice another cookie each. The dog remained on the blanket. I sat down in the recliner and picked up the remote.

"What is all that noise?" My father stood in the middle of the room.

The smoke alarm ceased its noise.

"Good, at least I can think now," said my father.

"Oh, Gabe, you're home." My mother entered the room and gave my father a kiss on the cheek.

"Of course I'm home. Carlos has good people working for him; they got me out of jail in a hurry."

"But now we owe Carlos money," said my mom. "Money we don't have."

My father put his arm around my mother. "Don't worry. Carlos said he'll just take out a little every week until it's paid."

"You going to keep working for Carlos?" I asked.

"Got to," said my dad. "Else how am I going to pay what I owe? You got an extra thousand?"

He couldn't possibly know. He's just guessing.

"Jade, I told you not to feed the girls cookies." My mother went over and took the cookies from the children. Patrice whimpered but neither girl cried. Guess they're as scared of my mother as I was when I was their age.

"Well, at least Jade came over to help while I was gone. Did you two get much done this afternoon?"

"Not much," said my mother. "Jade's only been here about ten minutes. Just long enough to feed the girls sugar and ruin their suppers."

"Jade just got here?" My dad looked at me. "Where have you been for the last few hours? I told you to come home and help your mother."

"Looks like things are under control here." I picked up my groceries and the bag containing my new underwear. "I've got to run."

MONDAY

MARCH 16, 2020

CHAPTER TWENTY-FOUR

FREYA

"WE NEED A NEW STRATEGY," SAID MARCY.

Back in the lawyer's office again, after Gabe got arrested. Of all the stupid things to do, Gabe does the most obvious and the most damaging. Of course, he thinks he has to support the family at all costs.

"What do you have in mind?" asked Gabe.

"This story has too many moving parts." Marcy pulled out a yellow legal pad and placed it squarely in front of her. She picked up a gold pen. "We need a simple story to tell the judge."

"Family's complicated," I said. "Especially our family."

"Then let's simplify things," said Marcy. "George Banks wants custody of the children." She wrote his name in block letters on the page. "So does Celeste, the biological mother." She wrote that down too, along with Jade and Carlos. "All these people want custody, and we have to prove that you are the best choice, over all the others or any other combination."

"Combination?" Gabe asked.

"What about Tracy Christensen?" I asked. "She's always threatening to take the girls from us."

"Tracy makes a lot of noise," said Marcy. "But she doesn't have standing; she's not a parent, and she doesn't have much of a case.

"But she could still screw things up." I can't get past that point.

"She can try." Marcy was tapping her pen on the desk. "But I can keep her out of the courtroom. I'm much more worried about other people's claims."

"Yeah," said Gabe. "What if people try to gang up on us?"

"Yes, Jade's original plan was to parent with Celeste. I think she realizes that's not going to work." Marcy crossed out Celeste's name. "Celeste lost her parental rights when Stella adopted Charity, and there's no provision for regaining them once lost. She may have some rights to Patrice, but Patrice isn't involved in the juvenile court matter."

"Celeste doesn't want Patrice," I said. "She dropped her off with us."

"Let's leave Patrice out of this for the moment." Marcy crossed George Banks off the list. "Banks isn't going to get custody either. Though he got a new trial on the drug charges, he brought a gun into the courthouse and no judge will overlook that."

Marcy turned the pad around so we could see it. "So that leaves Jade and Carlos. They could be viable candidates. They're younger than you, Jade appears to be clean, and Carlos is a local businessman."

"Carlos runs a bookmaking operation out of the cobbler shop."

I knew that was true, but it was the first time I'd heard Gabe say it out loud. He usually referred to it as "going to work" or "working with Carlos."

Marcy turned the pad around, to face her way, and drew a line down the middle. She labeled the columns "pro" and "con." Under pro, she wrote "age" and "businessman." Under con, she wrote "bookmaker" with a question mark.

"Which leads us to your arrest," she said. "Did the DA offer you a deal?"

Gabe looked up at the ceiling, out the window, and down at the floor.

So, I said it. "Gabe works for Carlos. If Carlos is arrested, Gabe will be too. The police arrested Gabe for assault on Jade, but he had lots of Carlos's money on him when they picked him up."

"Not good," said Marcy. "Please don't take this in the wrong way."

I've learned that whenever someone says that, it can only be taken in a negative way.

"There's no easy way to ask this." Marcy made some marks on the pad. "What Gabe does about Carlos, either way, won't look good. Have you thought of separating?"

"Separating? Like getting divorced?" This conversation was going in a direction I really didn't like.

"Yes, both Carlos and Jade have drawbacks as caretakers. Jade has a substance abuse and mental health history and, if we can prove it, Carlos is engaged in criminal activity." Marcy looked from Gabe to me and back. "But only Gabe has criminal charges pending. If you separated, Freya would be the best choice as caretaker, or guardian, of the children."

"No," said Gabe. "We've been together over forty years. We raise kids together."

"Are you married?" I looked at Marcy's fingers; a silver ring on her right hand, but no wedding ring. "How could you make a suggestion like that?"

Marcy leaned back in her chair. Under the overhead light, I could see grey in her hair. She looked older. "We are just exploring options," she said. "We need to talk about all the possibilities before we can decide what strategy works best."

"Not that one," said Gabe. "We stay together."

I nodded.

Marcy tapped the pad in front of her. "Then how can we prove Carlos has committed a crime?"

Gabe squirmed in his seat. "I know who his customers are; maybe one of them would turn on him."

"Maybe a customer that owes him money, wants to get out from under." Marcy made a note. "Do you know anybody who's not happy with him right now?"

Gabe looked up at the window and down at the floor. "No."

Marcy continued making notes. "Maybe we can use Jade's substance abuse history, her desertion of her family. Wish we had something more current though."

"Jade's had a hard life," said Gabe. "I don't want to make it tougher on her."

"In order to win this case, you need to prove that you can take care of the girls and that Jade can't. I can make a case against Banks and Celeste, but you need to help me on Jade and Carlos." Marcy put down her pen, folded her hands, and stared at a space between Gabe and me. "What do you suggest we do?"

"Maybe we need to talk about separating," said Gabe. "If it's the only way for the girls to stay with Freya."

"No," I said. "Absolutely not. We decided that wasn't an option."

"It doesn't look like we have any other options, hon."

Gabe never calls me "hon." Maybe it was a sign of how upset he was. He had to be out of his mind to think about us splitting up after forty years. There had to be another way.

Marcy stood up. "I think this conversation needs to take place without me. Why don't you discuss it and let me know what you decide?"

Gabe and I remained silent as she hustled us out of the office.

CHAPTER TWENTY-FIVE

GABE

Freya and I walked out to the car. I'd done it this time. Freya and I had agreed, years ago, that no matter what else we said, neither of us would talk about leaving unless we meant it. Now I'd brought it up in front of our lawyer.

I got into the driver's seat and Freya slammed the passenger door before she buckled her seatbelt. We both stared out through the windshield. I put the key in the ignition and turned on the car.

"What the hell were you thinking? Telling the lawyer that you would leave. What the fuck were you thinking?" Freya did know how to start a conversation. She never swore and she hated confrontation. That she's broken two of her own rules showed me how angry she was.

"What did you expect me to do? There's not many options left." I tried to keep my voice calm and soothing.

"Don't use that tone of voice with me," Freya said. "I'm not one of the kids who needs to be talked down to." Her voice got louder as she continued on. "I thought we'd agreed that whatever we did, we'd face it together."

"We've never been in this situation before." I turned to her. "I've been arrested and we may lose the kids."

"I know that." Her voice was almost a whisper.

I put the car in gear and drove out of the lot. Freya's silence lasted until the first stoplight.

"Sometimes you make me so mad," she said. "You have to support the family, your job gets you arrested, and now the kids may go live somewhere else."

The light changed and I started through the intersection.

She wasn't finished. "Why couldn't you just stay home and collect your disability? We would've managed."

"You know that's not true. If I didn't go to work, we wouldn't have enough money to raise the kids and we'd have lost them anyway. It's not like their parents can afford to raise them."

"That's why you can't leave now. I'm old. I can't work and raise two kids, and, if I don't work, I can't afford to raise the kids anyway."

"We've been through hard times before," I said. "We'll get through this too."

"Only if we stay together."

CHAPTER TWENTY-SIX

GABE

I PULLED INTO THE DRIVEWAY. AND ALMOST HIT THE CAR parked there. I was not in the mood for company. Standing on the porch was a woman, about forty, who could have used some hair dye. She carried a huge leather bag, stuffed with files. I knew immediately she was from the Department of Children and Families. They have a look about them.

Freya saw her too. "Be nice. And, whatever you do, don't talk about leaving the house."

We got out of the car. The DCF lady came over to us and shook our hands. Introduced herself as Myra Orestes. And started in asking questions.

"Can we go inside and talk about Charity and Patrice?" She started toward the house, as if it were hers, rather than ours.

I had a question of my own. "What happened to the last social worker we had, Lindsey Walker? She said she'd be out this month."

"Lindsey left the department," said Myra. "I've been assigned to your case."

Lots of people "leave the department." I don't know whether they can't hack the job, or there's a lot of firing going on over there. Myra is our fourth social worker since Charity was born.

Freya unlocked the door and offered Myra something to drink.

She said no, so we all settled into the living room. We had to push the Big Wheel and a stack of books out of the way to sit down. I meant to make Jade's old room into a playroom, but hadn't got around to it.

"When was the last time you saw your daughter, Mrs. Leary?"

"I only have one daughter, Jade, and she's an adult. I saw her a few days ago." Freya picked a piece of dog hair off the sofa.

"Celeste isn't your daughter?" Myra started flipping through the papers on her lap. "Celeste is the mother of both Patrice and Charity."

"That's right," I said. "Freya and I have only one child, Jade. She's the mother of the twins, Stella and Celeste, and she has a son, Christopher."

We had to go through the family history every time we got a new social worker. It took us several minutes to straighten it out.

"And so, when is the last time you saw Celeste?"

"A few days ago," I said. "I took her to urgent care."

"Was she injured?" Myra made some notes in her file.

"She had a burn," I said. "She showed up the next morning with a bandage on her arm. I got her some antibiotics."

Myra must have found her place in the file, because she rattled off the rest of the information. "You now have custody of Charity. Patrice, the other daughter of Celeste, is here with you now." She looked up. "What did Celeste say when she dropped off Patrice?'

"Nothing much." Not much I was willing to talk about anyway. "Said she had to get some stuff together and she wanted her to be in a safe place."

"And where is Charity right now?"

"Daycare," I said. "She goes three days a week, to be around other kids." DCF is big on something they called "socialization" that, as far as I can figure out, means kids being with other kids, playing.

"And Patrice?" Myra looked around, as if we had stashed Patrice in a corner.

"She's with a neighbor," said Freya. "We just came back from our lawyer's office. I'll need to pick up Patrice in a few minutes."

"Celeste has some learning disabilities, doesn't she?" was the next DCF question.

"Celeste sometimes doesn't understand what's going on. She gets frustrated." I knew that the DCF social workers liked it when you volunteered information.

"Mr. Leary, you and your wife raised Celeste and Stella also, didn't you?"

"Yup. Got custody of them when they were just twenty-two months old. Were their permanent guardians until they turned eighteen."

"You're not the guardian of Celeste now? Even with her learning disabilities?"

"Nope. You folks said she was doing fine as an adult. Didn't need us to be her guardians."

Myra stood up. "I would like to see where the girls sleep, if you would like to show me."

As I said, we've been through this before. They want to make sure somebody responsible is watching the child. Want to make sure we got supplies and a baby crib that is set up and safe. And smoke detectors and carbon monoxide detectors and a baby gate around the woodstove.

Freya went to show Myra around. Patrice and Charity slept in what used to be Celeste's room. It had a white crib and a toddler bed and ponies and clouds that Freya had stenciled on the walls. We had all the baby stuff—changing table and dresser and toys that beeped and whistled and did other educational stuff.

They came back into the living room.

Myra sat down, took a yellow pad and pen out of her bag and made a few notes. "Please sit down, I have some more questions."

Freya and I sat.

Myra looked directly at me. "Mr. Leary, you were recently arrested."

"Yes."

"For assault of your daughter."

"Yes."

"Can you tell me what happened?"

"No." This was not the time to volunteer information.

Myra put down her pen and looked at me. "What do you mean, 'no'?"

"My lawyer told me not to talk to anyone about what happened. She said it could come up later in court."

Myra picked up her pen. "I read the police report. There was a witness."

"Witness was mistaken."

"The department cannot allow children to remain in a home where there is domestic violence." Myra pulled a bunch of papers from her bag. "I would like both of you to sign this emergency action plan that I brought with me." She handed a copy to me and to Freya.

The paper said that Freya and I agreed to cooperate with DCF and sign releases so they could monitor services; these things were typed in. Then there were handwritten terms, probably added by Myra and her supervisor. They wanted me to leave and stay away from the home; I had to have a domestic violence perpetrator evaluation; Freya had to go to counseling for domestic violence victims; Charity had to remain in daycare and Patrice needed to be enrolled in a program. There were lines at the bottom for signatures. Myra had already signed it.

"Why do I need to go to domestic violence counseling?" asked Freya. "Gabe has never hit me or even threatened me."

"Your daughter has alleged that your husband assaulted her. We want to make sure you are aware of the signs of domestic abuse so that you can be prepared if it happens to you."

I couldn't stay quiet any longer. "Jade fell out of the truck. All the witness saw was Jade falling out of the truck."

"Jade said that you assaulted her. We believe victims."

Myra said this in such a self-righteous manner that I thought I might be capable of hitting her. This was getting out of hand.

"Charity has been with us her entire life. Never has anyone accused us of child abuse or domestic violence," I said. "Jade has a history of lying. And she lost custody of the twins because of what she did."

"What happens if we don't sign the paper?" asked Freya.

"Then I will need to call my supervisor and discuss removal of the children from your care."

She'd threatened to take the kids. Pull them out of the only place they'd ever been safe. "And put them with Jade?" I said. "With her history?"

I guess I spoke louder than I thought, because Myra stood up to face me. "That's a possibility," she said. "But, more likely, they will be put in foster care."

Charity and Patrice could go with strangers. Strangers who didn't know or didn't care that Charity needed her stuffed bunny to sleep or that Patrice needed to be watched every minute. I'd heard stories of kids being passed from foster home to foster home. What if Charity lost her stuffed bunny or Patrice didn't have her princess outfit? They'd be in a stranger's home with nothing familiar. And how would Freya and I know that they were safe?

I looked at the paper, then at Freya. Her face was colorless and her mouth was pulled in tight. She only made that face when she thought the kids or I were in danger.

I took the pen from Myra and signed the emergency action plan.

Then Freya did something I never thought she'd do. She took the pen and signed the plan.

CHAPTER TWENTY-SEVEN

JADE

THROUGH THE WINDOW, I SAW MY MOTHER SITTING AT the kitchen table. I knocked on the door. She stared at me for a full thirty seconds before she got up to let me in. Not that the lock could've kept me out; I'd worked the lock open with a credit card several times.

"What do you want?"

That was not like my mother, who invited everyone into her home. She stood blocking my way.

"I want to come in," I said. "I'm family; I'm not going to give you the new disease."

"New disease?" But she moved aside to let me in.

"Yeah, there's a new disease on a cruise ship." I sat down at the table. "Bunch of people have died."

"I've got my own problems." My mother sat down across from me. "Mostly because of you."

"Because of me? What'd I do? I just got here."

I looked around the kitchen. There's a picture of a princess on the fridge. Wonder which one of my granddaughters is into princesses. Seems a little sexist to me. And it's quiet; no kid sounds and no television.

"Where are the girls?" I asked.

"Out." My mother picked at the tablecloth. "Thank God." I saw tears form in the corners of her eyes.

I can't remember the last time I saw my mother cry. Maybe she cried when Stella died, but I wasn't around then. She got up to get a tissue and blew her nose. Looked like she'd been crying for a while.

"What's the matter? Is there something wrong with the girls?" Now she's got me frightened. What will I do if one of the girls has a disease or something? I'm not sure what to do.

"It's your father." She dabbed her eyes with the tissue. "He's gone."

"Where'd he go?"

"He moved out. Went to stay with friends."

My mom and dad not together. That's not possible. They'd got married to adopt me, and we'd had some hard times. But those were over and my parents were solid. Besides, it took both of them to watch the girls. I can't take them yet; I didn't get it squared with Carlos and my studio apartment is chaos now, to say nothing of adding two kids.

"You and Dad aren't together? When did this happen?"

"Just this afternoon. The DCF people were here."

That's even worse, if the DCF people took the kids. They may want to place them with me today. I want to be a grandmother, but this is moving too fast.

"When did DCF take the kids?" I needed more information.

"They didn't take the girls. Charity's at daycare, Patrice is with a neighbor." My mother made a vague gesture toward the street. "But, in order for the girls to stay, Gabe had to move out."

I don't say anything. That's okay, because Mom goes on talking.

"We had to sign a paper, saying Gabe had to move out and the girls could stay. Gabe signed and left."

That didn't make sense. I can't figure out what's going on. "Why now?" I asked. "You've been taking care of both of them most of their lives."

Mom got up, brought the box of tissues over to the table, and placed it in front of her. She grabbed a handful, looked at me, and blew her nose again. "He had to move out because he's been arrested. For assault on you. Kids can't stay in a house with domestic violence."

"Domestic violence?" The words came out before I could stop myself. I wanted a head start on custody, not my parents living in different places. Besides, even if I get custody, I'll need them to take care of the kids some days. In case I got a job or something. "It wasn't domestic violence. We had an argument."

"And you said he pushed you out of the truck. You said it to a witness and to the police."

I needed to say something. "I feel so bad."

"You should. And you should do something about it." Mom looked around the kitchen. "What did you come over here for, anyway?"

"It doesn't seem important now," I said. "I found out some things about that guy who came to court with you, Richard Fontaine."

"Found out something? About Richard?"

"Yeah, his father is a murderer. He was adopted by a murderer."

"That's not important now." Freya waved her hand with the tissue in it, like she's swatting flies. "What are we going to do about your father?"

"What about Dad?"

"He. Was. Arrested." Mom said every word like it was a separate sentence. "Because of what you said."

"I'll tell them I was mistaken," I said. "That we were arguing and I got out of the truck to avoid any more angry words. That's what happened, looking back on it."

"But, Jade, you need to think about things before you do them. Figure out what will happen when you do something impulsive."

We've had this argument before. I don't want to have it again, so I don't say anything.

Bong. Bong. Somebody's at the front door. Nobody who knows the family comes to the front door.

"I don't want to talk to anyone," said Freya. "Will you please see who's there?"

I went to the front door. A woman I'd never seen before was standing there. Not that I know many of Freya's friends, as I haven't been around. This woman was short, with a dark shirt and a long skirt. Her hair, dirty blond, tied in the back. She looked like a librarian.

I opened the door into the house and looked through the storm door. "May I help you?" That's what the folks on television say when they don't want someone in their house. I watched a lot of television in rehab.

"I'm Chloe Jay," she said. "I have an appointment with Mrs. Leary."

Not a librarian, a social worker. "Mrs. Leary isn't feeling well. Can I take a message?" I've got this part down cold.

"We had an appointment," she said again. "To talk about court tomorrow."

The custody hearing was tomorrow. Maybe I could get information from her. "What, specifically, did you want to talk about?"

"It's okay, Jade. I'll talk to her," said a voice behind me.

I turned around to see my mother, her eyes red but dry. She started toward the door.

The woman stepped into the house.

My mother, always polite, did the introductions. "Chloe, this is my daughter, Jade. Jade, this is Chloe from Citizen Advocacy. I'm sorry, Chloe, I forgot you were coming today."

"Citizen Advocacy?" That's where Richard Fontaine worked.

"Yes," said Chloe. "We provide advocates for community people who need a little help."

I turned to my mother. "What do you need help with?"

"Chloe is our advocate, to help us get custody of Charity and Patrice."

"Maybe I should be part of this discussion." I stepped back into the house.

"No, this is a private conversation." I saw my mother with my jacket in her hand. "You need to go."

She handed me the jacket and pushed me out the door. She's got lots of people on her side in this custody fight. But I've got some ammunition too.

CHAPTER TWENTY-EIGHT

FREYA

SOMEBODY ELSE IN MY HOUSE WHEN ALL I WANT IS TO BE alone. No, I don't want that either; I want Gabe home with me. Chloe looked at me for a minute and took off her coat.

"Are you alright?" she asked.

"Yes. No. Maybe." That about covered the options.

"What happened?"

"I'm sorry, I can't talk now. I've got to go pick up the girls." Charity was at daycare and they charged by the minute for late pickup. Patrice was with the neighbors. "I know we're supposed to meet before court, but I thought Gabe would be here."

"Where is Gabe?"

I felt the tears run down my cheek. I couldn't even think about it without crying. I'm not sure I'll be much use to the girls. But I'm all they've got now.

"He left." I went to the closet to get my jacket. "Can we walk and talk? I need to get the girls before daycare charges a late fee I can't pay."

"Of course." Chloe put her coat back on and opened the door. "Let's go."

Being outside calmed me down, even though it was only about forty degrees. Darkness was piling up and the world was white and gray. The snowbanks were dirty after multiple plowings, but the semi-darkness made them look soft. I started walking to the daycare, only a few blocks away.

"We need to talk about court tomorrow," said Chloe.

"I know. The DCF people were here today, causing trouble."

"What kind of trouble?"

We came to an unshoveled sidewalk. "We'll have to walk out in the street," I said. "Mr. Randolph never shovels his walk."

We both stepped into the slush by the side of the road. Only the top layer was slush; the slick ice lay just below.

"Wish we'd brought a flashlight," said Chloe. "It's dangerous walking out here."

I pulled my silver mini-light, about three inches long, out of my coat pocket and turned it on. "I've done this a few times; always keep a light in my pocket."

"I'm a teacher," Chloe said. "And I judge parents by how ready they are to overcome obstacles. You seem prepared for anything."

I didn't know how to respond to that, so I didn't. We came to the end of Randolph's property and had to scramble over frozen snow to get back on the sidewalk.

"What happened with Gabe?" asked Chloe.

"He got arrested," I said. "DCF said he had to move out or the children had to go."

"There must be another way to deal with this."

Chloe doesn't have children. Even if she hadn't told me, I could tell by that remark. Once the children left the house, it'd be hell to get them put back. We needed to do whatever was necessary so they stayed. "Didn't seem like it at the time."

We'd reached Charity's daycare. Only one car in the parking lot and three lights on in the building. I hoped weren't late. We entered the front door, into a hallway lined by cubicles where the kids kept their coats, boots, and school supplies. It was deserted. Gabe did most of the daycare pickup and drop off, so every other time I'd been here, the corridor was full of noisy kids, chattering and moving around. I hoped Charity was still here. When they removed her from Celeste, they got her at daycare and then told Celeste later. I looked at my hands and they were shaking. What if the DCF people decided Gabe was a danger and came and took Charity? How would I explain that to Patrice? Maybe the DCF people took both kids and didn't bother to tell me.

"Gramma, Gramma. You're late." Charity came running down the corridor, followed by a very young woman in a tight-fitting T-shirt. "I thought you forgot me."

It looked like I wasn't the only one afraid of being separated from my family. I knelt down and Charity put her arms around my neck.

The young woman came up and put her hand on Charity's shoulder. "Charity, I know you're excited to see your gramma, but you need to walk when you're inside."

Charity took her arms away from me and stepped back. "I'm sorry, Miss Emma." She looked around. "Where's Grampa?"

"Gramps couldn't make it," I said. "We need to get going."

"You're five minutes late," said Miss Emma. "That's a five-dollar fine."

A dollar a minute. I'll never make near that much money in my lifetime. I looked at Miss Emma; it's unlikely she's made that amount either, she was just the person sent to collect.

"I don't have five dollars," I said. "Can't we forget it, just this once?"

Miss Emma looked down at the floor. "I can say you made it just in time, just this once." She shifted from one foot to the other. "Besides, we're going to be closed tomorrow, anyway."

"Closed? But Gabe and I have to be in court tomorrow. We have to bring Charity here."

Chloe stepped forward. "Could there be emergency arrangements made, just for tomorrow?"

"No," said Miss Emma. "All the schools and daycares will be

closed tomorrow. We've been ordered to disinfect all places where there are children."

"Disinfect?" I asked.

"Yeah, the virus thing." Miss Emma moved her hand through the air, as if to push away the virus. "As a precaution, schools are closing and a special cleaning crew is coming in."

"What will I do with Charity while we go to court?"

"I'm sorry." Miss Emma did look sorry. "But you want the kids to be safe, don't you?"

I couldn't argue with that. Miss Emma seemed anxious to leave, so Chloe and I left with Charity. Charity didn't ask any more questions about Gabe, but she seemed to sense that something was wrong. She kept jumping off the sidewalk into the filthy snowbanks. It kept both Chloe and I busy, trying to herd her back on the sidewalk. At least I didn't have to talk about what happened today.

We approached the Magees' home, the neighbor where Patrice was staying. It was closer to home than the daycare, only two houses away. But we picked up Charity first because Lexie Magee didn't charge a late fee. Their walk was shoveled, with sharp lines, right up to the door. On the tiny porch, there was a shovel and sand, in case the walk needed further care. Lexie opened the door as we approached.

She led us down a hall with wood floors and pictures of the Magee children, all in identical frames. Patrice and Neil and Nathan Magee sat at the raised counter, putting together a puzzle. The dishes were all done and put away and the professional-looking cookware hung on hooks about the stove. The Magee house never looked like children lived in it.

Patrice looked at us and went back to what she was doing. Charity went over to join them.

"Would you like something? Coffee or tea?" asked Lexie.

"No, we're fine," I said. I introduced Chloe and Lexie to each other, both as "my friend." Didn't want to get into details.

"Lexie, can I ask you a huge favor?" Lexie lived to exchange favors, so I knew that was a way to get her attention.

"Sure, what gives?"

"Gabe and I have court tomorrow, about custody of the girls." I stopped to take a breath.

"I know," said Lexie. "I saw the DCF people at your house today. And the police a few days ago."

The joys of a small town. Everybody knew everything about your business. Nothing was private.

"Yeah, it's been tough," I said. "Anyway, Charity's daycare is closed tomorrow."

Lexie interrupted again. "I know; all the schools are closed. Did you see the lady from the CDC, said they might have to close the schools? I think she's being a bit dramatic; whoever heard of the schools being closed? She said she called up the superintendent of her kids' school and asked about his plans. He didn't have any. Besides, the president said we'll be fine. Just screwing up everybody's jobs, closing the school with no warning."

I knew Lexie would just continue to talk unless I stopped her. "Yes, it's tough," I said. "I know you agreed to keep Patrice, but I was wondering whether you could watch Charity too, just until we get back from court."

"No problem. Just bring her over with Patrice."

Charity and Patrice had grown bored with whatever they were doing, so it was relatively easy to get them into their coats and ready to go. We were standing by the door when Lexie called in the favor.

"Just before you go, could you do me a favor too?" Lexie pulled a blue-and-white box out from under the counter. "Neil is selling candles, as a fundraiser for band. Would you like to buy one?"

As I didn't pay Lexie, I bought something from every fundraiser her kids were involved in. I didn't need candles, and the cheapest was fifteen bucks, but I did owe her a favor. I didn't have fifteen bucks, but Chloe fronted me the money and paid for the candle. Now I owed her too.

TUESDAY

MARCH 17, 2020

CHAPTER TWENTY-NINE

GABE

W E'RE GOING TO COURT AGAIN. SEEMS MY NECKTIE gets harder to tie every time I put it on. It's the same suit I wore to court last week. That can't be helped, I only own one.

My fingers got tangled in the tie. I ripped it off my neck and threw it on the bed.

"That attitude won't get you what you want." This from Freya, standing in the bedroom door. "I know you're frustrated, but we need to do this."

Chloe had contacted some people, got permission for me to come home to get my court clothes. Maybe she'd be good to make some things happen.

Freya looked good, today in her wine-red dress. She had two dresses. Both looked good. One more court appearance and she'd start wearing the same clothes too. I know it's not about the clothes, but at least that's something I can control.

"I can't believe Jade did this to us. That she had me arrested." I went over to the bed and picked up the tie. "What was she thinking?" I put the tie around my neck. "I guess that's it, she doesn't think."

Freya stood in front of me and tied the tie. "Jade's had a hard life," she said. "Sometimes she doesn't think through what she's doing." She tied the tie as she talked. "She probably just wanted an advantage in court and then changed her mind. Realized she'll need us to take care of the children."

"But she doesn't think. She just makes things worse."

"Calm down." Freya patted the tie flat. "She doesn't trust anyone. She never has, not since she was left alone as a child. We knew that when we took her in."

"But then she has me thrown out of my own house. She's my daughter, I love her, but today I wish she wasn't around."

I wanted to talk more about the incident with Jade, but then we'd both be upset when we got to court. "But I haven't been arrested since I was a kid. And it's because of my daughter. That's not right."

"And we'll tell the judge that." Freya was using the voice she used to calm down the children. "It will work out."

No bus today, we don't have to go to Worcester. The Meredith courthouse is across from the municipal lot. Lots of parking and it's all free. I drove and Freya didn't say much on the way. Despite what she said, I think she's worried too.

The court parking lot was filling up, but we got there early enough to get a space. We went into the courthouse and through security. This place was much smaller than the main courthouse in Worcester, just two courtrooms and a clerk's office. It's four floors, but just a courtroom and a few offices on the top floors.

When we got to the third floor, a dozen people were already standing in the hallway. I looked around for Marcy Warner, our lawyer, but she hadn't arrived yet. I didn't see Jade or Celeste either. Freya went into the clerk's office. She's much better at dealing with the nuts and bolts of the system and is less likely to lose her temper. I leaned against the wall. Most of the people in the hallway looked under the age of thirty, even those that I assumed were the parents. Most of the older people wore suits, so I guess they worked for the court or were lawyers. Of course, I was wearing a suit and I'm neither. But I was brought up that you wear good clothes to court. Guess some of the young people didn't get that message. Most were in jeans and T-shirts. Some of the T-shirts had marijuana leaves on them and some had things I wouldn't even say, never mind wear on my shirt.

Marcy Warner, out attorney, showed up with Richard. He was on his scooter and having a hard time getting down the crowded hallway. Nobody wanted to move for him and a couple of people, including the guy with the marijuana leaf on his shirt, gave him dirty looks and muttered something when he passed. Guess his smoking didn't mellow him out enough.

"Let's go somewhere we can talk," said Marcy.

She seemed to know where she was going, so we all followed her to the end of the corridor, around the corner, and into an empty conference room.

She put her briefcase on the table. "This conference is for housing court; that's not in session today," she said. "Most people don't realize it's open."

Freya and I had followed Marcy into the conference room. Richard was having problems getting his scooter over the threshold.

"I'm sorry, but I have to speak to my client alone." Marcy directed this remark to Richard.

Richard stopped and looked up. "I have to tell all of you something important. And I want to do it in private." He started his scooter again and it cleared the door.

Marcy, Freya, and I stepped back. As there was little room between the table and the door, the scooter filled the space.

"Okay." Marcy went around the table, behind Richard, and closed the door. "You can talk to us, but I'm instructing my clients not to discuss the case in front of you. And I do need to see them alone, soon."

Marcy sat down across from Richard. Freya and I managed to squeeze into chairs also.

All eyes were on Richard. He was looking all over the room.

"This isn't going to be good, is it?" said Freya.

"This isn't about you. It's about me." Richard made some minor adjustment to his handlebars. "Your daughter, Jade, has been doing research on me."

"What did she find?" Marcy asked.

"She found out about my father."

"What about your father? Who is he?" I hadn't seen Marcy cross-examine anyone before, but I was impressed. And I didn't want to be on the other end of the questions.

"My father is Gerald Paoletti," said Richard.

It meant nothing to me, but Marcy sat back in her chair.

"Attorney Gerald Paoletti?" Marcy asked. "The lawyer on trial for killing a court clerk?"

Richard adjusted his handlebars again. "Yeah. He's my father."

"And Jade found this out?" I asked. "Did she contact you? What did she say?"

"She said she knew my father was a murderer. That my judgment was affected by my father's problems and I'm giving you bad advice."

"I didn't make the connection." Marcy took a paper and pen out of her briefcase. "How come your last name is Fontaine?"

"Gerald and Sylvia adopted me. After his arrest, I went back to my birth name." Richard shrugged. "It seemed easier."

"Easier than what?" I asked. Everybody in the room looked at me. "I think he should've told us."

"There's a DCF lawyer named Fontaine," said Marcy.

The confusion must have been on all our faces.

"I mean, everybody in the courthouse knows about your father. Sorry." Marcy didn't look sorry. "If Jade brings it up, we admit it and move on."

"That sounds good, we'll just move on," said Richard. "Chloe should be here anyway, and she'll be in court with you. Maybe it won't be an issue if I'm not there."

"Or maybe you have more than one conflict," said Marcy. "Is the DCF attorney your wife? I need to know that too."

Chloe knocked and opened the door, banging Richard's scooter.

"Chloe, come in," said Richard. "We were just discussing how to proceed."

"I just passed Jade in the hallway," said Chloe. She stood in the doorway, as there was not an extra inch in the room. "She has Celeste, all dressed up, and a man with curly hair with her."

"That's Jade's husband, Carlos," said Freya. "It looks like Jade is trying to get the whole family on her side." Freya turned to Marcy. "Jade told me that Richard's father was a murderer. I thought she was exaggerating."

Family is everything to Freya, so I know she's hurt. I leaned over and put my arm around her waist.

"Excuse me, but who are you?" Marcy directed her question to Chloe.

"Chloe Jay." She put out her hand and Marcy shook it. "I'm from Citizen Advocacy, here to help out Freya and Gabe."

Marcy turned to Richard. "I thought that was your job."

"No, I'm just the coordinator. Chloe will be going into court with the Learys."

Richard backed up his scooter a few inches, hitting one of the chairs. "If you folks would please move, I'll get out of here."

"You still haven't answered my question," said Marcy. "Are you related to Niagara Fontaine?"

"Niagara is my birth sister," said Richard. "I just met her, after not seeing her for over twenty years."

"And you took her name?"

"She's the only blood relation I have." Richard played with the controls on the scooter. "I'd rather have her name than my adoptive family's name."

"We don't have time to deal with this now," said Marcy. "Now, can I have a few moments alone with my clients?"

"One more thing before we go," said Chloe. "The woman Richard's father killed was my wife."

Nobody said anything for thirty seconds. I remembered that Chloe said she'd lost her partner, but I didn't know how tangled this was.

"And now you work with him?" asked Marcy.

"Yes," said Chloe. "Richard's a good man, not like his father. And I think my wife, Jenna, would have wanted me to do this."

Marcy took some more paper out of her briefcase. "Now, I do need to talk to my clients. Alone."

Richard attempted to back up his scooter and collided with the table. We pushed some chairs out of way and, with about a dozen attempts to turn, he got the scooter turned around and out the door. Chloe left behind him.

We all sat down at the table again. Marcy picked up her pen, stared at it for a few seconds, and looked up at us.

"The big issue is Gabe's arrest. That's going to be a problem," said Marcy.

"What about Richard and Chloe?" Freya asked. "Will that be a problem?"

"Probably," said Marcy. "But not a problem for today."

I wanted to argue with her, but didn't know what to say.

Marcy looked down at the paper in front of her. "Jade states that you were arguing, she grabbed the door handle and asked you to stop, and you pushed her out of the truck."

Freya looked at me.

I repeated my story for Marcy. "Jade and I were arguing. She opened the door herself, while the truck was still moving. I slowed down and she jumped out."

"There was a witness," said Marcy.

"A car stopped to pick her up. I don't know what she told him about why she was at the side of the road."

"The witness says that she came out of the door and rolled on the ground."

"I hadn't completely stopped. She lost her balance." I looked at Freya. "Jade makes up stories, she's done it all her life."

Freya remained silent.

"And there's an additional charge. You were found with proceeds from illegal gambling."

"Everything he tells you is confidential, right?" This from Freya. "You can't say what he said. Same as with me."

Marcy stared at her pen again. "What you're telling me is confidential and I can't repeat it. But if you get on the stand and testify to something different, I can tell the court I think you're not telling the truth or, more likely, withdraw as your attorney. When I withdraw, the judge will figure out why."

"So I'm okay as long as I tell you the story and you can bring in people to back it up? Then I won't have to testify."

"Whoa, wait a minute." Marcy put her pen down. "There are two cases going on: your criminal charges and your custody case. If you testify in the custody case, that testimony can be used in the criminal case. Illegal gambling probably will carry a longer prison sentence than assault and battery. Because the custody case is a civil matter, if you refuse to answer questions, the judge can draw a negative inference, or make a finding that you didn't answer the question because the answer is not good for you."

"I'm confused. Do I talk today or don't I?" I had other questions, but that was the first one.

"It is confusing," said Marcy. "Sometimes even for the lawyers. Let's take this one hearing at a time. For today, let me do most of the talking. If the judge asks you a question, answer it. Just answer the question. Don't tell a story, or start at the beginning; just answer the question. If the judge asks you about the incident with Jade, I'll say I've advised you not to answer because of the pending criminal charges."

"But if he doesn't answer, then we may lose custody of the girls. I don't want them with Jade. Or in foster care." Freya was almost in tears.

"That's unlikely to happen." Marcy picked up her briefcase. "Jade doesn't even have a place to live."

I noticed she didn't mention foster care. So I did.

Marcy put her briefcase back on the table. "Foster care is unlikely, especially with Judge Hartwell. She just got back from maternity leave, she wants to keep families together."

"Are you sure?" Freya took a tissue out of her pocket. "The DCF lady came to the house yesterday and made us sign a paper. Gabe moved out."

"What did you sign? Didn't I tell you not to talk about the case or to sign anything without talking to me?"

I was right, I didn't like being on the other end of Marcy's questions.

"We didn't have a choice." Freya dug a tissue out of her purse and wiped her eyes. "The DCF lady said that she'd take the girls with her if Gabe didn't move out."

"What did the paper say? What did you sign?" Marcy made some slashes on the legal pad in front of her.

Before I could say anything, Freya started rummaging through her purse again. She pulled out a paper, folded into four squares. "This is what we signed."

Even in all the stress and confusion, Freya amazed me. She knew what to bring and when to show it. Marcy unfolded the paper and made a few notes on her pad. "I can take care of this," she said. "Can I keep it?"

"It's our only copy," said Freya. "I keep it with me, to make sure to do what DCF said."

"This is outrageous and there's no need for it. I'll return the paper after court." Marcy slid it into the back of her pad. "After I ask the judge to give you both custody."

"Can we get custody, even if I move back into the house?"

"Nothing's for sure," said Marcy. "But Judge Hartwell is a predictable judge and she wants to keep children with family."

"But Jade is totally unpredictable." I didn't feel good about stating the obvious.

"And what about Tracy Christensen?" asked Freya. "She keeps threatening to do something so George gets custody."

"She's also not a problem for today," said Marcy. "I'll take care of her when she makes her move. But back to Jade, she doesn't have much to work with. No home, no job, missing for a year in rehab. But the judge may order visits with Jade. She may look at all the documents about her completing rehab and being clean, and order some contact."

Marcy put some more papers on the table. "I've been given all these documents about Jade's time in rehab, her clean drug screens, and her substance abuse treatment. It looks pretty convincing on paper."

"But Jade can't take care of a baby." Freya picked up the papers and glanced at them.

"She never shows up where she's supposed to be and she spends money she doesn't have. And how do we know this is all the records? That there aren't dirty screens and missed appointments she's not telling us about?"

"We don't," admitted Marcy.

"What about what's happened since Jade got back? She's buying Chris expensive gifts and I bet she bought Celeste's new clothes. Where's she getting the money for that? She's not working."

"Carlos may be paying for everything," said Marcy. "We'll ask him."

We walked out of the conference room directly into Chloe.

"Can we talk?" Chloe asked.

Chloe, Freya, and I went back into the conference room. Marcy left for court.

"What do you want to talk about?" asked Freya.

"Mostly, I wanted to keep you out of the hallway," said Chloe. "Jade is telling anyone who will listen that you've been arrested for assaulting her and for illegal gambling. The court officers seemed to be paying special attention."

"They escorted her out of the building the last time," I said. "She's quite good at dramatic entrances and exits."

"What about your arrests?" said Chloe. "Were you going to tell me about them?"

"My lawyer said I wasn't supposed to talk to anybody about the arrests," I said. "You could end up as a witness against me. Let's just say, Jade is trying to make it look as bad as possible. By the way, thanks for making it possible for me to be home this morning."

"And she's saying it as loudly as possible," said Chloe. "You need to ignore her, as much as you can."

"Yeah, after the last court appearance, my lawyer said I talked too much," I said.

"She said you interrupted her while she was making her argument." Freya took my hand. "You need to let the lawyers do their job."

"But it's so hard," I said. "They twist everything around, and believe Jade because she's younger and prettier."

"Let's stay in here for a while," said Chloe. "Marcy will come get us when we need to go into court and we won't have to deal with Jade."

Waiting is the hard part. We all know that important things will be decided today, but we can't do anything about it yet. Freya found a deck of cards on the windowsill and we played rummy. I lost, big time. I watched the clock, wondering if it was broken. Nope, the time matched the one on my watch.

"I'm going out into the hallway, maybe talk to Carlos," I said.

"Why Carlos?" Freya didn't sound like she cared.

I wanted to talk to Carlos, to ask him if he hurt Stella because she'd borrowed money from him and not paid it back. Even as I thought it, I knew the courthouse wasn't the place to have this conversation. Tina could have been lying, or could've been mistaken about Carlos lending money. Confronting Carlos here probably wasn't a good idea.

"I don't know," I said. "Maybe he can talk some sense into Jade."

"That's not a good idea." Chloe got up and stood between me and the door. "If you want to talk to Carlos, you need to do it after court. Right now, you're upset and frustrated at waiting and not at your best."

"I know." I sat back down. It was a dumb idea anyway. Carlos wouldn't hurt Stella, because he knew it would hurt Jade.

Marcy stuck her head in the door. "Time to go. The judge is waiting for us."

In juvenile court, each case was called individually, so we were the only people in the courtroom. If you don't count the judge, the lady that sat next to her and handed her things, the probation officer, and a court officer in a uniform. Judge Hartwell was an older woman, with gray streaks in her hair. Marcy said she'd just had a baby; she looked tired.

Judge Hartwell looked out over the courtroom. "We have a lot of people here. This is a closed proceeding; will everybody please identify themselves?"

"Attorney Montoya, and my client, George Banks. The petition is before the court because you granted Mr. Banks a new trial."

"Attorney Warner, and my clients, Gabriel and Freya Leary, who are the legal guardians of Charity Leary."

"Both father and the guardians are represented by counsel. What about the mother? Why doesn't she have counsel?" Judge Hartwell leaned over and conferred with the woman sitting at the smaller desk, to her right. "I have been informed that the mother, Celeste Leary, has had her parental rights terminated and her child freed for adoption. She does not have standing in this petition."

The court officer moved to the front of the court. Maybe she got some secret signal from the judge.

"Everyone else must leave the courtroom, except for Attorney Montoya and his client and Attorney Warner and her clients."

Jade popped up out of her seat. "Judge, I'm the grandmother,

Jade Vega, and I filed a motion for visits. I was told that would be heard today."

Judge Hartwell conferred with the woman again.

"Who is that woman?" I was careful keep my voice down when I asked Marcy the question.

She also whispered the answer. "That's Judge Hartwell's clerk. She's a new one, I don't know her name. She keeps track of the court record and checks on what's already happened in the case."

The judge looked up again. "You are correct, that motion will be heard today. And I've also been told that DCF has an interest in this matter. Attorney Hunter, for the department, and his client may stay in the courtroom."

I looked around. Myra Orestes, the woman who came to the house yesterday, sat in the back of the room, with a slightly-built man with salt-and-pepper hair. Until now, I didn't realize they were in the building. I turned to Marcy to say something, but she just put her hand on my arm and stood up.

"Your Honor." Marcy straightened her back and put her hands together. "DCF does not have custody in this matter and should not be a party."

She'd barely stopped speaking when the judge said, "Overruled. DCF filed the instant petition, years ago, and nobody else has been substituted as the petitioner. They will stay."

"Mrs. Vega, please leave the courtroom. We will call you back when we discuss visits."

The judge waved the court officer on and he cleared the courtroom. It took a few minutes.

"Mr. Montoya, we are here to set trial dates. Are you ready to proceed?" Judge Hartwell took a large black book and placed it before her.

"Your Honor." Marcy stood up. "I'd like to address a matter before we get to trial dates."

"I don't see your motion before me," said the judge. "Only Attorney Montoya's for trial dates and Mrs. Vega's motion for visits."

"Your Honor, this matter just happened yesterday and I'm hoping it can be addressed and resolved today. My client, Gabriel Leary, has been ordered out of his home by the Department of Children and Families. He is Charity's great-grandfather and has been providing care, during the day, for the child for years. More recently, Celeste Leary has left her other daughter, Patrice, with Mr. and Mrs. Leary. They have provided exemplary care, taken the children to the doctor and to daycare, and have provided for her every need. Just a month ago, after the untimely death of Charity's adopted mother, they were appointed guardians of Charity."

"I know that Mr. and Mrs. Leary have been caring for Charity," said Judge Hartwell. "What changed yesterday?"

"Mr. Leary was arrested," said Marcy. "His daughter, Jade Vega, accused him of domestic assault. Mr. and Mrs. Leary have been married for over forty years, he has raised his children and his grandchildren, and no hint of violence has been seen. Less than one week after Mrs. Leary comes back, after an absence of over a year, she accuses him of domestic assault for the first time in his life. The timing is suspicious."

The clerk handed the judge a paper. "This is the same Mrs. Vega that is asking for visits?"

"Yes," said Marcy. "My clients have concerns about that also."

"As do I. Attorney Warner, here's my suggestion. Please go out and meet with the Learys and Mrs. Vega and work this out. If not, I will hold a hearing and members of this family will be required to testify against each other. And you may not like my ruling. Do I make myself clear?"

"Crystal," said Marcy.

Attorney Montoya stood up and requested trial dates. Judge Hartwell scheduled them, with a statement that she hoped they wouldn't be needed. Attorney Montoya then asked for George Banks to have visits with Charity. The judge glared at him and said she didn't like sending a preschooler into jail, but that Attorney Montoya could be part of the discussion about visits. Looks like we may be here all day.

We went back into the same conference where we waited before. It was crowded, with Freya, me, Jade, Carlos, and Marcy. Thankfully, Attorney Montoya decided his client really didn't want to talk about visits and left.

Marcy started the discussion. "Judge Hartwell doesn't like family members testifying against each other, so she wants us to work out visits. The children are staying with Gabe and Freya."

"That's not fair," said Jade. "Carlos and I are younger and can take care of them better."

I'd had enough of this. "You don't even stick around long enough to see them. How do we know you won't take off again tomorrow? This time with the kids?"

"'Cause this time I'm going to parent with Carlos." Jade went over to Carlos, put her arm through his and leaned her head on his shoulder.

Carlos took Jade's hand, took it off his arm, and stepped away. "We're discussing it," he said.

"That's not comforting," I said. "What if Carlos had something to do with Stella's death?"

"Why would I want to kill Stella?"

"Because you lent her five thousand dollars that she couldn't pay back. And we all know what you do to people who can't pay."

The questions came, one after another.

"Why did Stella need five thousand dollars?" from Freya.

"Why'd you lend her that much money when you wouldn't give me even a few hundred?" from Jade.

"What the hell are you talking about?" from Marcy.

And the denial. "I had nothing to do with Stella's death," from Carlos.

We all glared at each other.

This was not going well. I put it out there. "Tina Watson said she and Stella were planning to move to Boston, to go to school. Tina said Stella borrowed five thousand dollars from Carlos."

Carlos sat down next to Freya. "She was going to take Charity with her, get a new start and a better paying job. The money was a gift, to help her do what she wanted. She's my stepdaughter. I didn't want to hurt her."

Carlos sounded convincing. Freya looked shell-shocked.

"This isn't getting us anywhere," said Marcy. "We were sent in here to settle the issue of visits. If you bicker like this in front of the judge, she may give custody to DCF."

"She can't do that," I said. "She already said we had custody."

"What if you all go in there?" asked Marcy. "Gabe says that Carlos may have killed Stella, Jade says that Gabe assaulted her. Freya's made it clear she doesn't want to parent alone and she believes Gabe over her own daughter. The judge may look at this mess and decide that DCF should figure it out."

"No, that can't happen," said Jade. "We need to keep the kids in the family. Even visits will be harder if they're with strangers."

"I'm glad you realize that," said Marcy. "A little collusion in this family will keep the kids where they are. Unless you really believe that the kids are in danger with anybody in this room."

We all looked at each other. I had to admit, I trusted family more than a stranger to take care of Charity and Patrice. Carlos and Jade were in agreement too.

"I don't want the girls to spend a lot of time with Jade until they get to know her better," said Freya. "And I want to know that Jade will stick around."

"That's fair," said Jade. "Let's start with shorter visits; then I can spend more time with the girls."

Everyone was being so reasonable; I didn't recognize my own family. We decided to start with two-hour visits on Wednesday afternoon, when Charity wasn't in daycare. We also agreed that Jade could spend time with the girls on Saturday morning, at our house. When we presented the plan to the judge, she approved it and we left the courthouse.

Freya and I were getting in the car when a slightly-built woman with dull brown hair approached us.

"Can I talk to you?" she asked. "I'm Danny Potts, a friend of Stella."

I didn't recognize her. The bouncy girl with red lips and ponytails had faded. She, Stella, and Tina Watson had been inseparable in high school.

Freya and I met Danny in front of our car.

"I wanted to talk to you," she said. "I heard you were talking to Tina and I wanted to see you."

"Why?"

"'Cause Stella and I talked the day she died. We were going to rent an apartment together, in Boston. Then my boyfriend wanted to get married, and stay here, and I didn't know what to do." She sighed and looked across the parking lot.

"What happened on the day Stella died?" Freya asked.

"Stella said she might be staying in town too." Danny put her hands in her pockets and put up her hood. "She said it might have been a mistake, taking money from her stepfather."

It was cold out here in the parking lot, and the wind was blowing over the open space. Danny didn't seem in any hurry to continue her story, but I wanted to know what she needed to tell me. I was going to ask her for more information when she started talking again.

"She said she didn't want to owe him anything, that it wasn't a good thing to do. She said she'd been talking to her mother and maybe it would be best for Charity and her to stay in Meredith."

"And?" I asked.

"That's it," said Danny. "But she seemed afraid of her stepfather, like she wanted to do what he told her to do." Danny pulled her phone out of her pocket and glanced at it. "I've got to go. I'm late for work."

"What about Tina's brother, Adam? How did he fit into this?"

"Stella and Adam broke up a few months ago. He was in Hartford the day Stella was killed." She looked at her phone again. "I've got to go."

I watched her go across the parking lot. My suspicions about Carlos all came back.

WEDNESDAY

MARCH 18, 2020

CHAPTER THIRTY

GABE

FREYA WAS TRYING TO GET CHARITY TO EAT HER BREAK-fast before she went on her visit with Jade. Jade's supposed to give her lunch, but we don't even know if Jade had money for food. On the other hand, Jade needed a chance to know her grandchild, if she was doing better. But Carlos was still around. Just thinking about it makes my head hurt.

It's good to be back home. Even with all the chaos and noise of my family. Of course, nothing was resolved. We still don't know how Stella died and I'm having second thoughts about this visitation agreement.

The girls are home full-time now. The daycare never reopened because of this virus. The television lady said it may be weeks before things are back to normal. It took both Freya and me to keep track of the girls. I don't remember it being this hard the first time. I know; I was fifty years younger then.

Charity threw her cereal bowl on the floor. She knew something was making us tense and she'd picked up on it. We tried to paint the visit with Jade as a great adventure, but I'm not sure we believe it.

"I'll clean it up," I said.

Freya didn't sleep much last night. She's got on the same clothes she put on yesterday, after court, and her hair was put up in one of Charity's hair ties. Maybe we are too old to be raising babies.

I took the roll of paper towels off the counter and leaned over to clean up the mess. My bum shoulder was bothering me, so I stood up and wiped the paper towel around the floor with my foot.

"That's not how you do it," said Freya. "You're just making a bigger mess." She leaned down to scrub the floor and Charity got out of her chair and tried to help her. Charity ran her fingers through the milk and picked up the cereal and put it in her mouth.

"Don't eat off the floor." Freya took the food out of Charity's mouth and wiped her face with a clean paper towel. "You know you're not supposed to do that."

Charity sniffled and wiped her eyes. Patrice started banging on the high chair. The paper towel Freya was holding was dripping wet and the roll had disappeared under the cabinet.

Freya looked at me. "Will you please do something helpful? Take the girls away from the mess or clean it up."

I picked up Charity and set her at the table. I gave her some dry Cheerios in a bowl. Freya retrieved the paper towels and finished cleaning the floor. She stood up and threw the towels in the sink.

I went over to stand by Freya. "I'm confused and scared about what might happen too." I put my arms around her.

"Charity is so young," she said. "And Jade is so easily distracted. What if she forgets to feed her?"

I tried to project a confidence I didn't feel. "It's only for a few hours, and now it's a court order. Besides, if Charity's hungry, she'll let Jade know. When was the last time Charity missed a meal?"

Freya doesn't laugh at my poor attempt at a joke.

"Can we watch *Clifford* now?" Charity had finished her cereal.

"When Bumpa's friend, Stan, gets here, you can watch while we talk."

As if conjured by Freya's words, there's a knock on the door. Stan's on the back porch and I let him in. After the girls are settled in front of the television, Freya, Stan, and I sit at the kitchen table. Freya offered breakfast, but we all settle for just coffee.

Stan put his leather bag, similar to mine, on the table. "I've run background checks on the principal players—Jade, Carlos, and Celeste. After some negotiations, I got copies of Stella's autopsy report, the report on the car, and the insurance investigations."

"What did you find?" asked Freya.

"No conclusions yet." Stan put the papers into neat piles on the table. "But I wanted to let you know what I've learned. The major problem is nobody seems to have a reason to kill, or even to injure, Stella. Murder is hard to prove without a motive."

"Let's start with Jade." Stan lifted one pile of papers and put it in front of him. "It appears she spent four months, less one week, in the Desert Recovery Center. She got glowing reports about how hard she was working. I couldn't get treatment notes or drug screens, but it looks like she was a success story. She left the program one week before her discharge date. That's unusual, but not unheard of. According to someone who was in rehab with her, she said she had to get back to her family."

"But Jade lies," I said. "She lied about me assaulting her."

"That's true," said Stan. "But I talked to two people who were in rehab with her and I sent the documents I had to her counselor, asked her if they'd been changed. She said no. It's hard to change every part of a paper trail."

"Jade might do it," said Freya. "What else did you find?"

"When Jade returned to Meredith, she rented an apartment on Beaumont Road. Lease is for three months, so she may not intend to stay there. I got a copy of the lease. Jade put down first month rent, last month rent, and security deposit. Two thousand four hundred dollars total. I haven't been able to verify where the money came from."

"That much money, landlord could still get stiffed if she stayed in the apartment and didn't pay," I said.

"Landlord thought of that too," Stan put a paper in front of me. "Landlord had Carlos guarantee Jade's rent."

"So they are a couple, even if they're not living together." Freya picked up the paper.

"Looks that way," Stan continued. "She spends several nights a week, overnight, with Carlos. He's next on the list. Carlos does bookmaking out of his shop. But you know that, because you're one of his runners."

Stan stared at me. I stared back.

"Carlos has a sweet deal going on. He stays in the shop, making like a cobbler, and has other people collecting his money. He declared a gross income of seventy-five thousand last year, about forty-five thousand after taxes. He may bring in two to three times that amount."

"Tina told me that Carlos lent money to Stella."

Stan nodded. "It may have been a gift, or it may have been a loan. Only Stella and Carlos know."

"So Carlos could've killed Stella because she didn't pay him back." I wanted this to make sense and this seemed the best possibility.

"Unlikely," said Stan. "Carlos can't collect money from a dead person. And, for the dozen or so years he's been running his own business, I can't find any other time he leaned on a client. Some of them had unexplained accidents and injuries, but nobody died. It doesn't seem logical that he would start with his stepdaughter. He could've just refused to give her money."

"If not Carlos, who then?" Freya asked.

"I couldn't find a viable suspect. Celeste is too messed up to do the planning and nobody else has a motive. Plus, it takes some expertise to sabotage a car. I'll keep digging, but so far it's been dead ends."

Another knock on the door. Freya got up and returned with Jade. She greeted Freya and me and stared at Stan.

"Hello, Stan," said Jade. "Haven't seen you in years. What are you doing here?" She looked at the papers in his hand. "You had me investigated?"

"Not you, specifically." Freya put her hand on Jade's arm. "Stan is investigating Stella's death."

"How are you doing, Jade?" Stan always had a special interest in her, because of his friendship with my brother.

"Okay, I guess. Why are you looking into Stella's death?"

"I need to know what happened to Stella," said Stan. "It's important to all of us."

"Funny you should share the information with my parents, not with me. You always told me I was like a daughter to you."

"I'll tell you the same thing I tell your parents," said Stan. "I've never lied to you."

"Good to know you're still on my side." Jade looked around the room. "Is Charity ready to go?"

The next few minutes were occupied in exchanging information, collecting Charity's things, and getting coats and boots. *Clifford* was finished, and Charity seemed willing to go. Patrice whined. Jade helped Charity put on her coat and boots.

I didn't want to ask the question, but I had to. "Is Carlos going to be with you when you visit Charity today?"

"No," said Jade. "He's working today. I thought the first visit should be just Charity and me. Not much planned; I thought we'd hang out at my house, get to know each other."

They left. I didn't know whether to be relieved that Carlos would not be with Charity, or apprehensive that Jade was going to take care of a child alone. I hoped Jade was telling me the truth.

CHAPTER THIRTY-ONE

JADE

THIS VISIT WASN'T GOING AS WELL AS I HOPED. CHARITY pouted and whined and let me know I don't do things like Gramma does. Mom said she's got some speech problems, but she seemed quite clear that she didn't want to be here.

She hated what she had for lunch. I've got it on good authority, from all my friends, that kids loved the lunch kits that come with cheese and crackers and meat and a drink, all in one package with some dumb cartoon character on the front.

"I don't like this." Charity pushed the lunch away. "I want fish stew."

What kid wants fish stew? "That's all we have for lunch." I put it back in front of her. "Eat it."

Charity got down from her chair, went to the refrigerator and opened the door. "Nothing in here. You don't got any good food and I'm hungry."

"Have some cheese." I picked the cheese out of the box and handed it to her. She threw it on the floor. "I don't want cheese."

"You'll eat what I give you." I guess I sounded serious, because that shut her up for about ten seconds. Then she started in, saying she's hungry. I took the lunch kit and put it in front of her. She knocked it off the table.

A knock at the door. Great, the neighbors were probably complaining about the noise. My first day with Charity, alone, and somebody may call the cops. But the knocking quieted Charity.

"Who is it?" No way was I opening the door in this neighborhood without knowing who was on the other side.

"Carlos." It did sound like Carlos. "And Chris. And lunch."

I opened the door. Carlos handed me a sack that smelled like fish.

"It's Charity's favorite," he said.

How did he know that? Chris pushed past me and went to sit by Charity.

"Can I come in?" asked Carlos.

"Might as well." I put the sack on the table. "How did you know that fish was her favorite?"

"I asked." Carlos took bowls and spoons from the cabinet. "I got enough for all of us."

I realized I was hungry. Taking care of a kid was hard work. Then I realized what he said. "Asked who?"

"Why, Freya, of course." As if it was the only thing to do. "Thought Charity could use something familiar on her first day here."

"Mom didn't mention anything to me." Not that she would, she doesn't want me to have Charity anyway.

"Did you ask?" Carlos spooned soup into the bowls. "She's trying not to interfere, but she'll help you if you ask."

"She wants me to fail." I don't feel so hungry now. "She wants Charity to stay with her."

"She doesn't want you to fail. She's just worried about Charity."

He waved his spoon in the general direction of Charity, who was now eating soup like she's starving. Maybe I needed Carlos's help in this parenting thing.

"I'm glad you're here." I tried the soup. "It's very good."

"I'm sure Freya will give you the recipe if you ask. Then you can make it when Charity comes over."

"Mom made the soup? Like, handled the fish and chopped the vegetables and stirred it on the stove?"

"That's the general way you make soup." Carlos took another spoonful.

Not for this girl. I'd seen my mother go through her all-day soup making when I was little, and all my soup came from a can. Or, the gourmet soup from Panera takeout.

"Gramma's old." Chris decided to join the conversation.

"No, she's not." Charity stopped eating long enough to point her spoon at Chris. "She's mature." Satisfied that she had defended her grandma, she went back to eating.

"Where'd she learn that?" asked Carlos.

"Probably heard my mother say it." Doesn't matter to me. "Mom said she's a good mimic."

"No, I mean Gramma is old and she wants you to take more care of Charity. That's what she told Grampa." Chris sipped his drink. "And Patrice too."

"Patrice too?" I echoed. What would I do with two kids? I remember the chaos when the twins were small. No sleep, no sex, no nights out. Maybe I could keep the kids some days but my mother never went out at night anyway.

"Don't you want both kids?" asked Chris. "You told me you wanted to take care of both kids."

"Yeah, of course I want the kids," I said.

At the same time, Carlos asked, "When did you tell Chris you wanted the girls?"

Chris looked down at his plate.

He might as well know. "Chris and I have been talking, even before I met him after the cemetery visit."

Carlos put his spoon down next to his bowl, looked at me, and asked, "How did you communicate with him?"

"I friended him on Facebook. Then I looked up his Instagram and Snapchat accounts. Started sending him little inspirational notes, telling him he was a good kid." Well, that's how it started.

"Is that all?"

I continued to eat. Carlos turned his attention to Chris.

"Well, Chris, is that all that happened?"

"Yes." The kid can't lie worth shit.

Charity threw her spoon at Chris.

"So, Mom, you said you wanted both girls. How come you only got Charity?" Chris picked the spoon off the floor and put it in the sink.

"I do want both girls," I said. "I just need to work up to it. Slowly."

"That's not what you said to me. You said you were ready for both girls right away. Why don't you take them?" Chris opened the drawer and gave Charity another spoon.

I got up and went over to him, like a good mother is supposed to. "It's okay. It'll work out," I said.

Carlos stood up. "Chris, let's be going. Charity probably needs her nap." He put the dishes in the sink. "And the social worker will probably come and check on you, Jade. You may want to buy some food."

"What kind of food? I got frozen dinners and burritos."

"Kid food," said Carlos. "Fruits and vegetables and cheese and fish stew, now that you know she likes it. Needs to look like you're ready to have her come home."

I haven't thought about food, what with all the hassles about toddler beds and child locks. Guessed that Charity would like what I bought for her or eat what I ate. But now I know better and may need to buy some stuff.

"I don't have any money," I said to Carlos.

"That doesn't surprise me." He laid a card on the table. "This is a gift card to Market Basket for thirty-five dollars. You give me receipts for thirty-five dollars' worth of groceries; I'll give you another card."

"You don't trust me to buy groceries for my own kid? What if I need something they don't have at that store?"

"Let me know and I'll pick up anything else you need." Carlos crossed his arms and stared at me.

I picked up the card. Maybe I can sell it for some other things I need.

"Remember, no receipts, no more cards." Carlos put on his coat.

"It's okay, Mom." Chris came and put his arms around me. "I know you can do this. I'll help you out, like I always do."

"Yeah, you're a good kid." I kissed him goodbye.

He wiped his cheek with his sleeve and Carlos and Chris left.

Charity started pouting as soon as they left. She threw the spoon that Chris just gave her, covered with fish chowder, at me, and so I got a white stain down the front of my only clean shirt. I checked the schedule that Freya gave me. Shit, it said right there that fish stew was her favorite. Like I couldn't care for the kid alone. It said she napped after lunch. Good, give me a chance to do some things I need to do.

Charity did look tired; she was drooping over the table. But when I suggested nap time, her head came up and she said she wanted to play.

"I'm tired," I said. "I want to take a nap."

Then I realized I didn't get a chance to buy sheets for her bed. Should've told Carlos I needed money for sheets and maybe I'd have more to work with. But I needed to put the kid down for a nap before we both lost it.

I looked around and saw the woodstove in the living room. It has a metal fence around it, about three feet high. The woodstove wasn't running, but I opened the gate and checked the inside. It's clean and the upright parts of the fence are about four inches apart. Charity can't get her head stuck between the risers and she can't climb the fence. Every fourth riser, the fence is anchored to the floor. If I put blankets and pillows inside the gate, Charity could sleep here and I'd know when she got up.

"Do you want to go camping?" I asked.

We spent the next few minutes getting out blankets and pillows and making a space to sleep around the woodstove. Charity lay down on the blankets.

"I want a story." She went to the bag my mother gave me, and came back with a book.

For the next twenty minutes, we read a story about an elephant and his friend, the pig, who share ice cream. Charity made me read it twice but, in the middle of the second reading, she fell asleep.

I have things to do, including getting the stain out of my shirt, so I leave her there. If she wakes up, I'll hear her before she can go anywhere.

I went into the kitchen, wet the dish rag, and tried to get the white goop off my shirt. Beside the sink is a half-full bottle of Xanax, left over from when my friend's grandpa died. I swallowed one to take the edge off. Snuck back out to the living area and Charity's down by the stove. Still asleep.

I decided to clean up, in case the DCF lady arrived. I washed the dishes and put the garbage in the bag. It'd been a while since I did garbage, the bag's overflowing and I'm afraid it'll break if I add much more. When I go to seal it, the smell hits me. I took it out to the dumpster to get the smell out of the house.

Tiffany, my upstairs neighbor, was coming back from the dumpster as I went out.

"Hey, I got in some new jewelry that you might like," she said.

Tiffany had some good stuff. Said it was because of her name; then she had to explain to me that Tiffany's is a fancy jewelry store in New York. She bought stuff online, she went to estate sales, and sometimes she had some really nice stuff, cheap.

"Maybe I'll be up and take a look." I threw my garbage into the dumpster.

"You'll need to look now, "said Tiffany. "It's going up for sale this afternoon."

Tiffany always gave me a good price because she doesn't have to ship it or pay money to anybody else that wanted a cut. Besides, I could use a few minutes of adult conversation.

I looked back at the apartment building. "Okay, but I've got to make it quick because my granddaughter's sleeping and I can't leave her long."

"You got your granddaughter back. Way to go." Tiffany and I did a fist bump.

"Not full time, but I'm working on it," I said. "And DCF is supposed to come sometime soon."

"We'll just sneak upstairs for a few minutes," said Tiffany. "If anybody comes, you'll be able to hear them on the stairs. It's not like we got great soundproofing or anything."

She's got a point. We went up to her apartment and I saw a necklace I liked. She wanted more than I had, and she wouldn't take the Market Basket card as partial payment. I left her apartment with nothing. Checked the parking lot before I went downstairs. No new cars, so the DCF worker wasn't around yet.

I heard Charity crying as I came down the stairs. Tiffany's right, you can hear everything from the staircase. Nobody outside the door, so she can't have been awake long.

It took me four tries to get the door unlocked. I wasn't going to leave her in the apartment with the door unlocked, I know that much, but she's crying so loud that I kept dropping the key.

"I can't get out. I'm stuck." Her voice got louder and clearer when I opened the door. Still, nobody showed up in the hallway.

I left the key in the door and hurried over to the woodstove. Flat on her back, her nose and face covered in snot. She'd managed to get her leg through one of the slats in the fence around the woodstove. Not just the bottom of her leg, but the whole thing up to her cooch. The layers of fat at the top of her leg prevented her from pulling it out again. Her thighs were red and scraped. My mother will be sure to say something when I bring her home.

"You left me alone," she said. "All alone. I was scared."

"It's okay, baby, I'm here now." I looked her over. She didn't seem injured, except for scrapes on her leg, caught between the uprights.

"I'm not a baby."

"Of course you're not. You're a big girl and we're going to get you out of there."

"I can't get out. I'm stuck." Charity started crying again.

I grabbed the pillowcase and tried to clean off her face. I needed to wash it anyway. "Okay, now we're going to get you out."

I tried squishing her fat rolls together, so that they fit back between the posts in the fence. Where did she get such fat thighs anyway? Must have been from her mother, because I still wear size four pants. I thought of picking up the fence, but the genius who made it put metal rods in the floor and I can't move the fence, up or down or left or right. Lifting up the fence just made her cry louder.

"Just suck it up," I said to her. "Leary women are strong." I went to the kitchen, got some kitchen oil and spread it on her leg. "This may hurt, but only for a minute," I told her. I twisted her leg to the left, pushed it back, and it slid out of the fence.

Charity looked like she was ready to cry again, but she said "Leary women are strong."

I hugged her and told her "Good job." I'm amazed it worked.

There's a knock on the door. With my luck the DCF worker should arrive about now. There's a purple bruise on her leg and it's covered with vegetable oil. I took the pillowcase and wiped off the oil.

"Anybody home?" A male voice I don't recognize.

I picked up Charity, wrapped the pillowcase around her legs, and carried her to the door with me. A bit awkward. She's small for a five-year-old, but still heavy, and she's still sniffling.

Standing in the doorway was Zeke, the kid from next door. His hair, blond with blue tips, hung in his face. He looked about seventeen, but I know he's old enough to drink in a bar.

"Thought I heard crying," he said. "Saw the door was open and I was worried about you." He looked around, as if a burglar would have stayed around through all the noise.

"No, just a mishap with the baby."

"I'm not a baby."

"No, you're not, so I'm going to put you down now."

He looked at Charity standing beside me.

"What happened to her leg? It looks rough."

Of course he would notice the bruise on her leg.

"I put her down for a nap, took off her pants," I said. "I'll get her dressed now."

Charity sat down on the floor and wouldn't move. At least she's quiet about it.

"Thanks for checking on us." I tried to close the door on Zeke.

"I want a popsicle." That from Charity.

"I'd like a popsicle too," said Zeke, pushing his way back into the apartment.

Was he five years old too? What's the big deal about popsicles?

Charity stood up and started jumping up and down. "Popsicle, popsicle, popsicle."

"I don't have any popsicles," I said.

"We could go to the store and get some." This from Zeke, not Charity.

Maybe I can get us out of the apartment and get some shopping done too.

"Can we go to Market Basket?" I asked. "I need to get some other things for Charity. Do you have a car?"

"I have my truck," said Zeke.

"I like riding in Bumpa's truck." Charity continued dancing around.

"But I don't have a car seat," he added.

Car seat? I don't have a car seat because I don't have a car. But I wasn't staying here any longer than I had to.

"Does your truck have three seatbelts? We could strap her in, she's tall enough. It's only a few minutes to the store, I just don't want to haul the groceries home."

Zeke looked at me and then at Charity. Maybe he really wanted the popsicles. "We could put her between us. But you'll have to pay attention, make sure she doesn't get into anything."

I was sort of hoping for some adult conversation, or at least conversation with Zeke, on the ride. Can't have everything and I needed to get out of this apartment. "Okay, let's do that."

Charity seemed happy to be leaving too, and tried to help me put on her pants and shoes. A minor hassle over her jacket, but she put that on too. Zeke hadn't used all three seatbelts in a while, so we had to dig them out and get everybody strapped in. Charity insisted that Zeke and I use our seatbelts, if she had to. At last, we're on our way.

"What do you need to get?" asked Zeke.

I guess that's as close as I'm going to get to adult conversation.

"Some cereal, milk, bread. And popsicles." I adjusted my seatbelt; it's digging into my neck. Charity seemed fine with hers. "I got a gift certificate from Market Basket."

The drive's uneventful and we got a parking spot near the door. I hated grocery shopping, but Zeke's a label reader and Charity seemed happy in the riding car attached to the grocery cart, so I decided to enjoy the time out. I picked up what I need and some cookies and whoopie pies, in case I needed to bribe Charity later.

When we got to the checkout, the total was $50.35. I dumped my purse out on the checkout. Moved things around.

"Something wrong?" This from Zeke.

"I can't find the Market Basket card," I said. "It was in my purse earlier today." I moved the lipstick and the tampon holder to the side.

Zeke looked over the contents of my purse. Like most men, he doesn't touch anything.

"I can't find it." I put everything back in my purse and started going through my pockets.

Charity said. "I want my popsicle."

I squeezed a few tears out of my eyes.

"I'll pay for the food," said Zeke. He put a debit card into the reader and pressed in the code.

"Thank you, thank you so much." I wiped my eyes with my finger. "I don't know what else to do."

"That's all right; I'll take care of it." Zeke even pushed the cart to the car.

We're loading the groceries and putting Charity in the car when an older woman unlocks the next car over.

"Do you have a car seat for the child? She's supposed to have a car seat." The woman came around the back of her car to see into ours.

"It's in back of the seat. Didn't want somebody to take it while we were in the store."

My explanation seemed to satisfy her. Anyway, she got into her car and drove away.

Zeke, Charity, and I pulled out of the parking lot and went by the liquor store.

"Would you like some adult beverage, instead of that popsicle?" I considered leaning over and touching Zeke when I asked the questions, but Charity's between us.

"I thought you didn't have any money."

"I want a popsicle," said Charity.

"I don't." I looked out the window. "But I thought maybe you'd buy something for us."

"You shouldn't drink if you're taking care of Charity." Zeke continued past the liquor store without even slowing down.

Everybody thinks they have a right to comment on my parenting.

We spent the rest of the short trip home in silence. Zeke helped me carry the groceries to my apartment.

"Do you want your popsicles now?" I asked.

Though I hadn't directly asked him, Zeke answered. "No, I think I'll go home." He pulled open the door. "You should lock the door behind me." He left.

"Need to pee," said Charity. She started to pull down her pants. The bruise on her leg looked bigger than when we left for the store.

I followed her into the bathroom.

"No, no," she said. "Get out." She tried to close the door.

"I need to look at your leg," I said.

She pulled down her pants. The bruise is purple and swollen and will probably look worse tomorrow. I'm definitely going to hear from my mother about this.

As if summoned by my thoughts, a text came from my mother. "Started supper. R u planning to feed Charity before you bring her home?"

"I'll feed her." Give me more time to see if I can do something about the bruise. I remembered I used to get ice when I got bruised, so I check the freezer. One tray of ice, one bag of mixed vegetables, and one of frozen chicken. I took out the bag of mixed vegetables and put it on Charity's leg.

THURSDAY

MARCH 19, 2020

CHAPTER THIRTY-TWO

GABE

THE DAYCARE WAS CLOSED. NO REOPENING DATE HAS been set, but the president said this won't last long. I don't want another day like today. The girls woke up early, demanding breakfast. When they were told they would have to eat at home, and they wouldn't see their friends, the whining started.

Patrice threw her orange juice. The cover came off the sippy cup, and it spilled all over Charity's eggs. Charity wouldn't eat the eggs with the orange juice on them, so I did. They were soggy.

While Freya was making more scrambled eggs, Charity got out the Cheerios and the milk.

"What are you doing?" I asked

"Making breakfast." She poured the milk into the bowl. I've told her millions of times not to pour the milk, but she didn't spill a drop. She picked up her spoon and started shoveling Cheerios into her mouth.

"Don't you want eggs?" I asked.

"You eat them," she said.

"Eggs, eggs, eggs." This from Patrice who was feeling left out.

Freya put the eggs down in front of Patrice. She ate them with her fingers. I tried to interest her in the fork, but she was having none of it.

"I wanna watch TV," said Charity.

"Finish your cereal."

She picked up her cereal bowl and proceeded to the living room. Freya stepped in front of her, took the bowl, and put it on the counter.

Charity wailed. Patrice took the fork she'd ignored before and banged it on the highchair. Clang, clang, clang. The chair had gone through four generations of Learys, but now I wished we'd bought a plastic one, rather than sticking with the metal one.

"Stop." When Freya said it, we all stopped. "What would you be doing now at daycare?"

"Weather," said Charity.

"Make stuff," said Patrice.

"What about the weather?" asked Freya.

"We see what weather is outside. We put sun and clouds on the board." Charity looked around, as if we might have a weather board in the kitchen.

Freya disposed of the breakfast debris and wiped everything down. No weather board, but we got paper and crayons and drew pictures of sun and clouds. After a short squabble over who got the blue crayon, and Freya miraculously producing not two, but three of them, the girls settled down.

"We need to go shopping," said Freya.

"We just went a few days ago. What do we need?"

"Hand sanitizer, and disinfecting wipes, and toilet paper."

"What do we need that stuff for?" I'm not a neat freak, but we had cleaning supplies.

"The man on the TV said we needed to sanitize surfaces, wash our hands, and wipe off everything we bring into the house."

"You worry too much."

"TV, TV, TV." Patrice stopped coloring at the mention of her favorite activity.

"No TV now," said Charity. "We need to go outside and see the weather."

It was March, so that involved coats and scarves and boots. Charity yelled when I put on her boots.

"Does your leg still bother you?" I pulled down her pants. The bruise was still purple, but was turning green and yellow around the edges.

"Gramma Jade left Charity alone." Charity pulled her pants back up.

"Gramma Jade left you alone?" Freya asked.

"She went outside, left me alone. I got stuck and cried. But I'm not a baby."

We'd gotten very few details from Jade. But it sounded like she left Charity alone, if only for a few minutes.

"Then what happened?" I asked.

"Tried to go with her. She left me in a cage. Couldn't get out."

"In a cage?" This from Freya.

"She came back." Charity pulled on her other boot. "Then Gramma Jade and me and Eek got popsicles."

"Who's Eek?" asked Freya.

"What about the cage?" I said.

"Eek got me popsicles. Grape and cherry." Charity came over to stand in front of me.

I zipped up her coat.

"Want sicles," said Patrice.

"Let's go outside and look at the weather," said Freya.

I didn't have a better idea, so we went. The girls ran around the yard and looked at the clouds.

"Do you think Jade left her alone?" Freya asked me.

"I don't know. But I want to know who Eek is and what's the cage she's talking about."

"She's only five." Freya looked up at the clouds. Checking the weather, I guess. "She could get it wrong."

"Maybe we should call Marcy," I said. "It costs every time we talk to a lawyer, but I'd just like to check things out with her."

I thought Freya was going to say no, but then she said, "We'll wait until the girls go for a nap. Then I'll go to the market, and you can call Attorney Warner."

It seemed a long time until they napped. We spent some time outdoors, then we made macaroni necklaces, and then lunch had to be made. It took three times the usual effort, with both girls trying to help. At last, it was naptime. Freya left to get cleaning products and I sat down to call Attorney Warner.

I thought I'd have to leave a message, but she answered the phone.

"I'm glad I got you," I said. "I'd like some advice about Charity."

"Is there something wrong with Charity? Is she alright?"

"She had her first visit with Jade yesterday," I said. "She came back with a bruise on her leg."

"How did she get that?"

"Don't know." I stood up. I needed to move if I was going to talk about this. "Charity's bruise looks really bad and Jade didn't even tell us about it. Just dropped off Charity, three hours after she was supposed to."

"Children often get bruises," said Marcy. "It may be nothing."

"But Charity said Jade left her alone and then she talked about somebody named Eek who bought her popsicles. If the first visit went like that, it may get worse."

Marcy sighed. "The reason I'm in my office today is because the courts are closed until further notice. I suggest you talk to your daughter and see what she says about the visit."

"If she did leave Charity alone, can we get back into court?" It seemed like the whole world was panicking because of something we couldn't even see.

"The courts are closed. Emergencies only. And unless you can prove that Charity is in danger with Jade, it's not an emergency."

"So we have to work it out ourselves."

"At least for the next few weeks, until the courts open again."

There wasn't much else to say, so I said goodbye.

CHAPTER THIRTY-THREE

FREYA

I SAT DOWN AT THE TABLE, ACROSS FROM GABE. BOTH girls were still asleep, but we needed to get some things settled. I poured two cups of coffee and set one in front of him.

"We need to talk about Charity," I said.

"You mean we need to talk about Jade." He looked down at his coffee cup.

"Charity had bruises on her when she got home last night." I took a sip of coffee. Too hot. "After she got home, three hours late. Marcy says the courts are closed and it's not an emergency."

I knew kids got bruises, but the one on Charity's leg was large and she cried when I touched it. Jade hadn't mentioned it when she dropped her off.

"What are we going to do?" I stirred my coffee. "Maybe we should try to work out something with Jade, to keep the kids safe."

"That worked out so well the last time you tried it." Gabe wasn't even trying to spare my feelings, but he was right.

"What do you suggest?" See if he had any better ideas.

There was a knock on the front door. I heard a dog bark.

Gabe went to the door and returned with Chris. And Alaska, who put his nose on the table.

"Alaska, down." He sat at Chris's command.

"What are you doing here on a school day?" asked Gabe.

"School's closed." Chris went over and poured himself a cup of coffee. "They're cleaning everything, because of the virus. It's a big deal." He took off his jacket, hung it on the back of the chair, and sat down at the table with us. "Do you have any boxes?"

"What kind of boxes?" I asked.

"Moving boxes," Chris said. "Mom's moving in with us."

I don't know whether that's a good thing or a bad thing. With three of them together, they might watch Charity and Patrice better and she won't get any more bruises. Or Chris and Carlos may be so busy dealing with Jade that nobody will watch the girls.

"Where are Charity and Patrice?" asked Chris.

"Asleep," said Gabe. "They closed the daycare too."

"They say it's going to be bad." Chris finished his coffee in a swallow. "Schools may be closed for weeks, maybe longer."

"They're not going to close the schools," said Gabe. "Never been done before, why start now?"

Chris ignored him. "So, you got any moving boxes?"

"I think I've got some downstairs." Gabe got up and went to the cellar door.

"No, Grampa, I'll go down and get them." Chris opened the door, flicked on the light, and disappeared down the wooden steps.

Alaska went over to the door and sniffed the threshold.

"Don't worry, old fella," I said. "He'll be right back."

Alaska sat by the door.

"Carlos and Jade are going to move in together." Gabe shut the cellar door. I don't know whether it was to keep the heat upstairs or to prevent Chris from hearing us.

"Looks that way," I said.

"You think they're trying to make this work or is it just a way to get the kids away from us?"

"I'm sure I don't know." I really don't know what to think, but I'm positive I don't want to talk about it.

"The judge seemed to buy the argument that we're too old." Gabe picked the coffee cups up off the table and put them in the sink. "She gave visits to Jade without really thinking about it."

The cellar stairs creaked and Chris opened the door. The door hit Alaska, who moved over to the side. Chris was carrying several cardboard boxes with the words "Marlboro" and "Salem" on the side. He put them down on the kitchen floor.

"How come you got so many cigarette boxes when nobody smokes?" he asked.

"Celeste used to work at the KwikMart. She got the boxes to hold her stuff and just leaves them here between moves," I said.

"Good thing she moves a lot," said Chris. "I don't have to go all over the place to get them."

Chris put on his coat and clipped the leash on Alaska. "Thanks for the boxes." He picked them up and left.

We heard a car start.

"Does that kid have a license?" I asked.

"Don't know," said Gabe.

"He's breaking the law. He could get into serious trouble if he's caught."

Gabe looked out the window at the car going down the street. "We all did dumb things when we were kids." He turned around, walked over to the table, and leaned down.

"This must have fell out of Chris's pocket." Gabe showed me the phone in his hand.

"Jade bought him one of the new, fancy smartphones," I said. "That's what's called a flip phone, just for talk and text."

Gabe flipped open the phone and pressed some buttons. "Lots of calls and texts, but mostly between Chris and Jade, I guess. Go back over a year, talking about when she'll come home and what's going on around here." Gabe pressed some more buttons. "Even Chris seems to think we're too old to be raising toddlers."

"What are you going to do with it?"

"Give it back to Chris next time I see him." Gabe put the phone in his pocket. "Probably not tell him I read his messages."

CHAPTER THIRTY-FOUR

GABE

I NEED TO TELL FREYA WHAT I FOUND IN CHRISTOPHER'S phone. Not the fancy phone that Jade bought him, but the flip phone that fell out of his pocket. At first, I convinced myself that I wouldn't invade his privacy. Then I thought I'd find out what he was saying to his mother, and what she was saying to him, for his own good. Then I read how much he missed his mother, put the phone away, and vowed not to take it out again until I gave it to him.

Like so many other times in my life, I didn't keep my promise. I love Jade dearly, but I know she is a bad influence on her children. She claimed she bought Chris the watch and the exercise bracelet, but I know she doesn't have any money or any income. And there's the bruises on Charity's leg. I couldn't take the chance, so I finished reading the texts between Chris and his mother. Thought I'd made a mistake in what I read; that they must have talked in between and changed things. But Jade is not one to provide a strong moral compass.

I had to tell Freya.

The best time was later, in the evening, but it seemed like forever before it got dark. Chris came back once more for boxes, and I was afraid he'd noticed his phone was missing. Then the girls wouldn't go to bed; they kept asking for snacks and stories and shooting questions at us to prolong bedtime. It was almost ten before Freya and I settled into our chairs in the living room. Before Freya could turn on the television, I laid the phone on the table between us.

"What's that?" She picked it up. "Isn't this Chris's phone?"

I looked into her eyes. She knew whose phone it was.

"Why didn't you return it to him when he came to get more boxes?" she asked.

"Maybe I should have," I said. "But I want to talk to you about what's on it."

She turned it over. "What's on it?"

"The text messages," I said. "I read them."

"Why did you do that?" I could feel the disappointment in me across the room.

This was going to be the hard part.

"I wanted to know what Jade and Chris said to each other, before she came home. Jade isn't a good influence on him."

"And that justifies invading his privacy?" She put the phone back on the table.

"Yes," I said. "I know you don't want to hear this, but I'm worried about what Chris might have done."

She got out of her chair, put her arms around her body, and walked over to the window. "Do I want to hear this?" I asked.

"Probably not."

She turned around to look at me. "Tell me anyway."

"Right before school break, Chris starts telling Jade it's time to come home. He says he knows the family will need her soon. Then, after Stella dies, he tells her she has to come home now and take care of the family. He says he made it so she could get custody of Charity."

She turned to look out the window again. "Is that all?"

I got out of my chair and went to stand beside her. "What do you mean, is that all? Isn't it enough? Right before we work on the car, he tells her she has to come home and then he takes credit for bringing her home to get custody. We've got to do something about this."

"Maybe Chris just feels guilty. He thinks he's responsible for Stella's death." She walked away from me and sat back down in the chair. "Though I guess that's bad enough, if he thinks he's responsible."

"No," I said. "The text reads: 'I fixed it so you can come home and take care of Charity. Don't tell Grampa and Gramma.' Then later, 'Stella's dead and now you have to come home.'" I looked up from the phone. "Jade may take advantage of his guilt." I regretted that statement as soon as I said it. Freya didn't see Jade the way I did. "I mean, if he did it."

"I don't think she'd do that." Freya gave the predictable answer. But she didn't stop there. "Either way, I think we need to talk to Carlos and Jade about it."

"Before or after we discuss custody and the bruises on Charity?" It was a nasty thing to say, but I was getting tired.

"We'll do both at the same time." Freya sat down and picked up the remote. "We'll settle all the family issues in one meeting."

I think her faith was misplaced, but I don't argue.

FRIDAY

MARCH 20, 2020

CHAPTER THIRTY-FIVE

JADE

CARLOS AND I WENT OVER TO MY PARENTS' HOUSE TO discuss custody of Charity and Patrice; Chris insisted on coming with us. Said he's part of the family too. Just when I was making some progress, they shut down the courts and I'm back talking to my parents again. Not that they're bad people, they take good care of the girls. They just don't know how the world works and they keep getting us mixed up with the Department of Children and Families. The department is unreasonable.

We all sat down at the table and Freya gave us coffee and cookies.

"Where are the girls?" I asked, looking around. Their stuff was scattered all over the kitchen and living area. Kids are messy.

"The neighbor is watching them." Freya put out the sugar and milk. No cream. "I thought it'd be better if we're not interrupted while we talk."

"Is it safe to have them at the neighbor's when they can't go to school?" I asked. "You know, the virus thing."

"I trust that the neighbors are healthy," she said.

Of course, she trusts everyone. There were a few minutes of silence while everybody did something to their coffee and picked out a cookie.

Gabe looked at me, then Carlos. "Are you and Carlos going to be parenting together?"

"Yes," I said.

"No," said Carlos.

"Well, that clears it up." Gabe stirred the coffee he'd already stirred before.

"Carlos is going to help me," I said. "We just haven't decided whether we're going to live together. Most of my stuff is at his house."

Thankfully, Carlos doesn't say anything.

"So how do you see this working out?" Gabe took the spoon out of his coffee and laid it on the table.

"How about if the three of you become co-guardians of both Charity and Patrice?" Carlos asked it just like we'd rehearsed.

"How will that help us?" asked Freya. "We can't agree on anything now."

"We can have a written agreement about when the kids stay where, just like a rental agreement," I said.

"A rental agreement?" This from Gabe.

"Bad example," I said.

Carlos gave me the evil eye. He wanted to be in charge.

"You mean like a parenting agreement?" Gabe asked. "Like they spend the week with us, we get them to school and appointments, and they spend Saturday night and Sunday with you."

I don't think I want to give up my Saturday nights out. "How about they spend Wednesday and Sunday with me? That way, they can sleep in the same bed every night." I sounded like a good grandmother, worried about shuffling the kids around. "I would like to be invited to any sports or school events, even if they're not on my days." I've got this grandmother thing nailed.

"Can you take care of Charity? She came home with a bruise."

Great, they wanted to talk about this now. "I didn't have a bed for Charity, so I put down some blankets and had her sleep inside the fence around the woodstove. The stove wasn't going and I thought she'd be safe there."

"You put her in a cage?" asked Freya. "Like an animal."

"No," I said. "I made it up nice, put blankets and pillows. It was comfortable. I laid down with her, read her a story."

"How did she get the bruise on her leg? It's raw too, like she struggled to get away from something."

Leave it to my father to figure that out. "I went outside to take out the garbage. While I was out, Charity woke up and tried to get out of the fence. She caught her leg between the uprights. I checked before I left, she couldn't get her head through them."

"Why was Charity not in the bed we bought her?" asked Carlos.

Even he was ganging up on me. "I didn't know how to put it together."

"Let's leave this aside for a moment." My dad placed a flip phone on the table. "We need to talk about this."

I picked it up. "What? A flip phone?"

I saw Chris check the pocket of his jacket. "That's my phone," he said.

"I bought you a new phone," I said.

"I know." Chris picked up the flip phone. "This is the one I bought, to talk to you."

My father turned to me. "You've seen the messages on this phone?"

"Yeah," I said. "Chris sent them to me."

"Grampa looked at the messages on my phone." He stood up. "They're private, between my mom and me."

"I agree your grampa shouldn't have looked at the messages, but it's no big deal." I'm trying to support my son. "Is it?"

Chris took a step back from me. "But we worked so hard to get custody of Charity," he said. "And Patrice."

"We're going to share custody. Five days with Bumpa and Gramma, two days with me," I said. "You can see her when you want to."

"But that's not what you wanted." Chris sounded like he was five years old himself.

Carlos came up to Chris and put his hand on his shoulder. "Calm down. It looks like this might work itself out."

Chris's voice got even louder. "But this isn't what Mom wanted. She said she'd come back if she could have a family and get custody of Charity."

"If you didn't know whether you were coming home, why did you talk about getting custody of Charity?" Carlos asked.

Damn, he was always good at asking questions that I didn't want to answer.

"Chris wanted us to be a family," I said. "We talked about that a lot."

"And she said that Celeste deserved a chance to be a mother, and that she could come back and help out Celeste and we could all be a family." Chris was almost in tears.

"I wanted us to be a family," I said.

"You said it wasn't fair to Celeste, just because she had special needs, to be deprived of Charity. You said Stella stole Charity from her mother." Chris said this without taking a breath.

I don't want to think of either of my daughters as bad mothers. I'd made some mistakes myself, but I hoped to help my kids do better.

"But the messages say more than that," said Gabe. "Chris says that he's taking steps so that his mother can come back and get custody of the girls."

"You said Celeste deserved to have her kids," said Chris. "You said you'd come back and help her if she had Charity."

"But she didn't have Charity." I pointed out the obvious.

"But you said you'd come back if she did." Chris's voice cracked, from emotion, I guess. "And I made sure she had the chance." Chris stopped talking, as if realizing he'd said too much.

Carlos picked up on it immediately. It took me a moment to realize what he'd said.

"How did you make sure she had the chance?" When Chris

doesn't answer, Carlos came out from behind the counter and stood next to him. "How?" he demanded.

"I…. I meant." Chris stopped talking, looked around the room, ran for the door, yanked it open, and went outside.

"Do you know what the hell he's talking about?" Carlos asked me.

"Not a clue."

Carlos came over to me and grabbed my arm. "Tell me the truth. What's he talking about?"

"I told you, I have no idea." I shook off his arm.

He crossed the room and went outside. I didn't see Chris, but Carlos looked both ways, turned left, and set off down the street.

That left me alone with my parents.

Freya got up and started clearing off the table.

"I guess I shouldn't have had Chris lie to his father." I stood up to help her.

"More than that, you encouraged him to think you'd come back if the girls needed you," said Freya. "So he took steps to make that happen."

"Like I said to Carlos, I don't know what he means."

Freya stopped and stared at me. I guess I'd only told her partial truths too many times; she doesn't believe me now.

"I. Don't. Know."

Carlos came back, dragging a reluctant Chris with him. He set Chris in a chair at the table. "You stay there," he said. He picked up two chairs and placed them across from Chris.

"Sit." He pointed at me and at the chair.

I sat. So did he.

Carlos took a deep breath. "Tell us what happened."

"I didn't mean to." Chris burst out crying. "She was only supposed to get hurt, so she couldn't take care of Charity."

"Who is she?" I asked the question, though I'm pretty sure I knew the answer.

"Stella." He cried harder.

I got up, went to the counter, and came back with a box of tissues. I handed him a few and kneeled down beside him and put my arm around his shoulders.

"I only wanted her to crash, to get hurt." Chris blew his nose. "She couldn't take care of Charity, and Mom would come home and help Celeste." He stared at the tissue in his hand. "I didn't mean for her to die. She always wore her seatbelt and cars are supposed to be safe."

We all stayed where we were for a few seconds. Even Freya stopped moving around, cleaning things up. Then my knees started to hurt, so I stood up and sat back in my chair.

"What do we do now?" That from Carlos, always the practical.

"I'm going to jail, aren't I?" Chris asked.

"No, you're not," I said.

Freya sat back down. Gabe didn't move.

Carlos looked at me. "We can't promise that. Stella's dead."

A plan was beginning to form from the thoughts racing around in my head. "Only we know that," I said.

Carlos shook his head. Chris stared at the floor.

"He's our kid, we have to protect him." I directed that remark to Carlos. "I know I've made mistakes as a mother, but I'm not letting him go to jail. Are you?"

"No." Carlos didn't sound convinced, but he gave the answer I wanted.

"What about you?" I directed the question to Gabe and Freya.

"He's not going to jail," said Gabe.

"He killed his sister," said Freya.

"But he can't go to jail," I said. "He needs a chance to grow up."

"What chance did Stella get?" I can't believe my mother's not on my side.

"Stella's dead," said Gabe. "There's nothing we can do about that."

"Stella's dead, and that's forever," said my mother. "Chris can't just walk away."

"But we can't let one bad decision, no matter how awful, ruin his entire life." My

father looked directly at my mother. "We need to protect him, like I was protected."

"We can work this out," I said. "The police have been investigating for a month and they haven't made any progress or any arrests. They've barely talked to Chris, so they don't suspect him." This sounded better as I said it.

"But they have questioned me and your parents. They are still looking at the family," said Carlos.

"But it's not on the top of their list," said Gabe. "They don't really suspect any of us. They didn't even question me about it when I was arrested."

I'm surprised my father could pick up on where we're going.

"That's right." I put my hand on Chris's shoulder. "They don't suspect us and all we need to do is lie low and it will all go away."

Carlos stood up and started pacing back and forth. Chris and I watched him for a few seconds.

"You're going to let him get away with this?" Freya's voice went up an octave. "After he killed your granddaughter?"

"He didn't mean to do it," said Gabe. "He's young and he didn't know. He deserves another chance."

I can't believe my father is making this argument.

"That's right," I agreed. "He didn't mean to do it."

"No, I didn't." Chris put his head on the table, so the next words were garbled. "I only wanted to give Mom a chance with Charity. I didn't mean to kill Stella."

"He kills Stella and nothing happens to him?" This from Freya, but I can tell she's coming around to our way of thinking.

"Yes, something happens to him. He has us on his back, every minute, every day, for the next few years. We know where he goes, who he sees, and what he does." Gabe crossed his arms. "He won't have a chance to screw up again, and we'll save one of the grandchildren we still have."

"I think you're right," I said. "But why are you doing this?" I'm glad he was, but I still don't understand why my father was agreeing to it.

He uncrossed his arms, put his hand on the table and took a deep breath. I think he's not going to answer me.

"Because," he said. "Because, when I was young, I did something foolish, put somebody in danger." He took another breath. "It worked out, but it made an impression on me. I never did anything to purposely hurt anyone again."

I couldn't imagine anything he did that was bad. He's talked about his life, his dreams, and I never heard about a bad thing he did. I asked him.

"I left you alone," Gabe said. "For four days, alone in a snowstorm."

I remembered the story from my childhood. How my parents were killed in a car crash and I was home alone. Five years old, I survived for four days.

"I was alone because my parents were killed in a car accident," I said. "You weren't even around; you were in Vermont with Freya."

"We were in Canada." As if that were the most important part of his statement. "It was my first weekend alone with Freya. I couldn't wait for it to begin."

"How were your responsible for my parents' car crash? They were on the way home from the hospital. My mother thought she was having labor pains, but she wasn't, so they came home." I'd heard this story dozens of times while I was growing up.

Gabe got up and poured himself another cup of coffee. As if he needed something to finish the story. "Ever wonder why your parents didn't take you with them to the hospital?" he asked.

"It was snowing. They didn't expect to be gone long." Again, I'd heard this as part of the story; I have no memory of their leaving. Only flashes of being alone, eating snow, and being so scared.

"Does that sound like your parents?" Gabe sat down again. "Were they the kind of people that would leave you alone?"

"I don't know," I said. "I never got to know them."

"And that's my fault," said Gabe. He stared into his coffee cup. "I was supposed to be there, watching you. I was, but I left twenty minutes early to go pick up Freya."

"What are you saying?" I don't want to believe what I think I heard.

"Your parents were on their way home, just twenty minutes out," said Gabe. "I was twenty years old and anxious to be with Freya. I left you alone and went to pick her up. It was only twenty minutes."

Freya took Gabe's hand. "In those twenty minutes, your parents died and you were left alone. We were in Canada—this was before mobile phones—and we didn't know what happened until we got back."

"You knew about this?" I can't believe my mother knew and never told me.

"Gabe's mother and I backed up his story," said Freya. "Nobody ever knew."

"That's why we need to protect Chris." This from Gabe. "He can't let one mistake stop all the good he may do in the future."

I was furious at Gabe and Freya for fucking up my life, all those years ago. I can't believe I got conned into working out an agreement with them after his complete disregard of me. And I'm aware that I need him to prevent my son from going to jail.

"You fucked up my life," I said. "And I am so pissed at you. But I need to protect my son." I put my hand on Chris and Carlos and head to the door. "This is not over yet."

My dramatic exit was screwed up because we needed to get our coats and other stuff. But we left and my parents knew they needed to watch out.

CHAPTER THIRTY-SIX

JADE

WE DON'T TALK ON THE WAY HOME. CHRIS SAT IN THE back seat and played with his phone. I should probably take it away from him, if we're going to enforce the part about being up in his life. But I'd activated the GPS on his wristband, and he wore it all the time. I'm not looking forward to the conversation when we get home.

We got out of the car and Chris followed us into the house. Carlos and I took off our coats.

"I'm going to go out," said Chris.

"No, you're not," said Carlos. "We need to lay down some ground rules. We need to know where you are."

"I made one mistake, and you're going to punish me for years? I'm out of here."

"You killed your sister." Carlos went over to take hold of Chris's arm. "And that can't be undone."

"I didn't mean to. It was an accident."

"Accident or not, she's gone," said Carlos. "And you are going to stay at home until further notice. You can't go anywhere anyway, the stores are closed. You need to learn to follow rules."

"Yeah, because this family is so good at following rules. Like Mom follows the rules about mothers not leaving their children.

And you follow the rules about illegal gambling. Let me do what I want, or I'll have you arrested and Mom reported, and I'll go live with Buzz and his family."

Carlos looked like he was going to hit Chris. Not that he'd ever hit either of us, but there's always a first time.

"Okay, maybe we shouldn't talk about this now." I went over to Carlos and separated him from Chris. "Chris, go to your room. Your dad and I need to talk."

To my surprise, Chris obeyed. Though he slammed the door on his way.

"I can't believe this." Carlos sat down. "The kid threatened to get me arrested."

He also threatened to turn me in as a bad mother. Don't know where he gets these ideas.

CHAPTER THIRTY-SEVEN

FREYA

GABE AND I SAT AND STARED AT EACH OTHER.

"What do you think she's going to do?" Gabe asked.

"I don't know," I said. "But I don't think we're going to like it."

I needed to do something, so I went and got the bag from the cupboard and put it on the table. I pulled out the first rune. For once, Gabe didn't object.

"No, not like that," said Gabe.

"Why not like that? I do this every week, just to check on how we are doing."

"I know." Gabe resumed his study of the table. "Do the circle thing, the full reading, not just checking in."

"Okay."

I cleared a larger space on the table and let all of the runes slide out of the bag onto the table. Then turned them all over so that the carved surfaces were not seen. I picked up the first rune.

"This is the guide," I said. I didn't know how much Gabe remembered about the divination circle, and talking through it helped me too. I turned over the rune. Wynn.

"That's Jade's rune, isn't it?" asked Gabe.

"Yes," I said as I placed it in the upper right-hand corner. Wynn is often translated as "glory." I remembered Jade, coming to us at five years old; I immediately dubbed her glory. Since then, I've learned not to assign runes to children until they are older.

"Jade is our guide?" asked Gabe.

"I don't know," I said. It was tough to imagine self-centered, impetuous Jade as a guide. "But she certainly seemed determined to influence our lives."

I slid another rune toward me. Laguz, the formless and unknown. This symbolized the immediate past. Then Eihwaz, our foundation, a stone of strength and stability. I placed the Laguz to the left of the circle and Eihwaz at the bottom.

"What do those mean?" Gabe was always impatient, wanted things to happen now.

"The foundation rune is strength and stability. That's what you bring to the family." I smiled at Gabe. "The Laguz means an uncertain past. I won't be able to tell you the complete story until I finish the circle."

I placed the next rune on the top of the circle before I turned it over. "This is the rune of our desires and dreams." I turned over the Naudhiz rune. "Unfulfilled dreams," I said.

"That's bad."

"Not necessarily. We all need dreams that are a little out of our reach, they keep us going." And sometimes they pull us down.

I took the final rune from the bag. Turned it over immediately. Gyfu.

"Gyfu," I said. "A gift." I placed the rune to the right of the circle.

"We're going to get a gift?"

"Maybe, but maybe not so literally." I picked up the rune again. "It's a rune that often comes with sacrifice."

Something tinged in my head. My mind was making connections that I wasn't aware of. That was our life, sacrifice and gifts. I looked at my husband of over forty years.

Family is complicated.

ACKNOWLEDGMENTS

Once again, I have been gifted with people who want me to succeed and who have helped me bring this book to publication. Many people read and commented on sections of the book but Diane Kane, Elizabeth Tennessee, Mary Ann Faughnan, and Ann Forcier read the entire manuscript and provided valuable feedback. Steven and Dawn Porter, and the group at Stillwater River Publications, used their expertise to make this a better book.

And, as always, I have to thank my family. My mother and my sister kept asking me when I would finish writing and when they could hold an actual book. My grandchildren, Alex, Abbi, and Brent, all at different stages in their lives, encouraged me with their potential. They have endless possibilities, due to their parents, Tina and Tony. This book is dedicated to Tony, my son, who is entering into new adventures himself.

MAY I ASK A FAVOR...

Reviews and discussions about books matter to an author. While it's nice to be recognized, reviews and discussions let publishers know the importance of supporting authors and continuing to put out books.

If you liked this book, or even if you did not, please consider leaving a review on your preferred social media or inviting me or any other author to your book club or local library. If you have questions, comments, or want to chat about the book, contact me through my website; you can also sign up for my newsletter there.

jamcintosh.com

Made in the USA
Middletown, DE
27 October 2023

41348538R10150